Coyote Terror

Range detective Rance Dehner arrives in Conrad, Texas, for a few days of fishing and finds himself in the midst of treacherous Indian trouble. Akando, who heads a band of renegades, has demanded that the town bans Indian children from attending its school. He threatens that if his orders are defied, Conrad will be attacked by Coyote, a mythical man/wolf of Indian lore.

Angie Knowland, the schoolmarm, is determined to keep the school open to all children and is supported by Sahale, the tribal chief. But a series of gruesome murders terrifies the townspeople and leads to explosions of violence. Dehner must protect the school and uncover the real culprit behind the killings as hatred, fear and gunfire ravages the small Texas town.

Coyote Terror

James Clay

A Black Horse Western

ROBERT HALE

© James Clay 2020
First published in Great Britain in 2020

ISBN 978-0-7198-3133-1

The Crowood Press
The Stable Block
Crowood Lane
Ramsbury
Marlborough
Wiltshire SN8 2HR

www.bhwesterns.com

Robert Hale is an imprint
of The Crowood Press

The right of James Clay to be identified as
author of this work has been asserted by him
in accordance with the Copyright, Designs
and Patents Act 1988

Typeset by
Simon and Sons ITES Services Pvt Ltd
Printed and bound in Great Britain by
4Bind Ltd, Stevenage, SG1 2XT

CHAPTER ONE

Reverend Nate fidgeted nervously as he listened to the music being performed by the church choir. They sounded good, for a collection of ranchers and homesteaders, but he had to admit that most of his attention was focused on the pianist, Angie Knowland. What would she think if he confessed that his interest in her went beyond planning the music for the Sunday services and Wednesday night prayer meetings?

And how would the rest of the congregation handle it? These were good people who had accepted a lot. Was he asking too much? Yet he was a lonely man, and…

The music ended. Reverend Nate silently rebuked himself. A pastor shouldn't spend Sunday morning agonizing over personal problems. He got up from his chair on the church platform and quickly walked to the pulpit, which stood in the middle of the platform in front of the choir loft.

He smiled at the group of about seventy-five people sitting on wooden pews. He opened a large bible to the place where he had tucked the red ribbon that served as a marker. 'Our scripture this morning comes from…'

The church's two front doors made a banging sound as they were shoved open, and an arrow flew through the small building, burrowing into the pulpit. Screams filled the air as a group of sixteen Indians entered, forming a line along each side of the church. Their leader remained standing just inside the doorway, holding the bow that had made the shot. The rest of the Indians were carrying rifles: new and shiny and pointed at the people sitting in the pews.

Reverend Nate gestured with both hands for the congregation to remain calm. He walked to the front of the pulpit, yanked out the arrow in a defiant gesture and threw it to the floor. The clergyman then stepped off the platform and walked up the center aisle toward the man who had fired the arrow.

The Indian holding the bow spoke in a mocking voice as he walked to within a few feet of the pastor. 'The white man's Spirit has little power. Akando can scare his people with only one arrow.'

'Akando speaks with a forked tongue,' snapped Reverend Nate. 'Akando does not come alone. He brings many braves, all carrying guns. Akando knows the people of the book never bring weapons into a church. A church is sacred ground.'

'Nata has learned the ways of the white man well. He has even taken a white man's name. He has forgotten his family, who are now with their ancestors because of the white man.'

Reverend Nate breathed deeply and held in his anger. 'My family was killed in a tribal war by other Indians. I was orphaned at the age of eight. A man of the book and his wife adopted me and raised me as their son.'

'They taught you the ways of the white man.'

'They taught me that violence begets violence. Those who take up the sword perish by the sword. Akando would do well to heed such wisdom.'

Akando's eyes took in the tall, middle-aged man with a craggy face who now stood a few feet behind Nata. The man was named Shem Carson. He was the town marshal. Like Nata, he was unarmed, and, like Nata, still dangerous.

'We have come for a purpose,' Akando abruptly proclaimed. 'You will stop teaching Indian children in your school. You have until what you call the first day of October to do what Akando demands. If not, this town will be destroyed and all who live in it will be killed.'

Shem Carson took a step forward. 'Akando, as far as I'm concerned, you and your so-called braves are nothin' but a band of outlaws. You are renegades. The chief of the Wichita, Sahale, has given permission for Wichita children to attend school. Sahale is a man of honour and his word carries a lot of weight. The words of a renegade don't mean a thing. If you try to make good on your threats, a passel of soldiers will come and stop you.'

Akando's smile was broad and vicious. 'The soldiers will need much time to journey here from the nearest fort. If you do not do as I say, when the soldiers arrive they will find dead bodies and ashes.'

A lanky, elderly man with a grizzled face suddenly stood up in one of the pews and shouted, 'Stinkin' redskins, we'll kill ever one of ya!'

Another man stood up directly behind the shouter and placed a hand on his shoulder. 'This is a time to remain calm, Leo, please sit down and allow the marshal and the pastor to continue their discussion with our unexpected guests.'

Leo appeared confused by the well dressed man who smiled pleasantly as he spoke, but he took the suggestion and sat down. The well dressed gent nodded politely at the men standing in the aisle and then resumed his place on one of the hard pews.

Akando seemed angered by the polite gesture. 'The man who threatened Akando will die. Until Wichita children are set free from your school, the town will feel the strength of Akando.'

Anger filled Reverend Nate's eyes and his voice was accusatory. 'Will Akando, who calls himself a mighty warrior, kill an old man?'

'Akando will not have to do the killing.'

While his face betrayed no emotion, a chill gripped Reverend Nate. The confidence of total evil now filled Akando's eyes. The pastor found himself without a voice.

Shem Carson's words broke the silence. 'Who is going to do your killin' for you, Akando?'

The leader of the renegades looked directly at the man he still called Nata, where he knew his reply would be understood: 'Coyote.'

Angie Knowland gave a light laugh from where she sat at the piano; several children giggled along with her. Reverend Nate looked at Akando with a silent, stony expression that was a stern warning.

Akando turned and walked out the door, his band of outlaws following after him. The last one to depart fired a shot, shattering a window in the side wall of the church.

CHAPTER TWO

'Never mind the window!' Reverend Nate shouted over screams and shouts as he returned to the platform and stood beside the pulpit. 'We will turn this service into a time of prayer...' The clamour continued, and Nate shouted once again, 'Please, let us have order!'

Marshall Shem Carson said nothing, but waved his hands at the congregation in a 'calm down' motion. The lawman sat down in the front pew as an uneasy quiet settled over the church.

Howard Dixon, a pot-bellied man who was the owner of the Lucky Ace Saloon, stood up from a middle pew. 'Before we start all this prayer business, I got me a question, Reverent.'

'Yes, Howard?'

'What did that Injun mean when he said, "Coyote"?'

'Can I answer Mister Dixon's question, Reverend Enders?' Angie spoke from the left side of the platform where she sat in front of a battered piano. She always called the clergyman by his last name, though he preferred the less formal Reverend Nate. The pastor hoped she was only acting out of the habit of being respectful.

'Yes, of course, Miss Knowland.'

Angie gave a comforting smile to the congregation, all of whom appreciated it. 'As most of you know, I am a school teacher. Coyote is a delightful creature in stories the Wichita tribe tells to its children. The Indian children bring the stories to school with them, and all of our children love those tales.' She looked directly at the mothers in the congregation. 'I know many of your children have told you these stories.'

Several women in the congregation managed slight smiles. A fragile sense of ease began to waft over the assembly.

But Reverend Nate had to destroy it. The people of Conrad, Texas, could be in for a hard, bloody assault. They must be prepared for it.

'What Miss Knowland just told you is true,' the pastor said. 'But there is another meaning to Coyote, and one I'm sure Akando intended.' Reverend Nate paused, then decided that to hold back would be dangerous. 'Coyote is a monstrous creature, half human, half creature of the wild, who kills like a savage wolf.'

Frightened voices crackled like wildfire through the small church. Howard Dixon once again sprang to his feet. 'You gotta stop this right now, Reverent. You're an Injun, go to Akando and tell him the school will be closed to Injun kids, startin' right now.'

'I can't do that,' came the reply from the pulpit.

Dixon wasn't about to give up. 'Why not?! You're in charge of the school. The folks who adopted you started this whole mess.'

Nate inhaled and privately counted to ten before continuing in a controlled voice. 'My adoptive parents ran a mission school originally for Indian children only. Conrad is located close to the Wichita reservation. After my parents died, it was decided to combine the mission school with the school here in Conrad. The mission agency continues to pay part of the expense.'

Howard Dixon's anger spiked and his voice rose. 'But this church pays half for the school. It's our money! You're a redskin, Pastor, but we've been good to you, and you owe us. Go tell Akando we'll do what he says, we won't let no more Injun kids...'

A loud, unmelodious chord filled the small church. A rash of startled cries was followed by all eyes turning toward the platform.

Angie Knowland stood up at the piano whose keys she had just pounded. She shot an intimidating look at the saloon owner, who immediately sat down. Angie then glared at the rest of the congregation and declared: 'It's bad enough that you are all behaving like despicable cowards! But you expect our pastor to crawl like an insect too? Reverend Nate owes us nothing but to proclaim the truth. It is the truth that will set us free, not a lot of sniveling nonsense.'

A quiet fell over the church. Reverend Nate looked at the pianist. His smile was one of gratitude. He returned his gaze to the congregation. 'I think we're ready to pray now.'

*

Leo was still sober as he gulped down his final drink of the evening. Sam, the owner, wiped perspiration from her forehead as she returned the bottle to a shelf directly behind her, and then placed the glass Leo had emptied into a container under the bar.

'You've been paid your day's wages, Leo,' she declared loudly. Everything Sam said was in a loud voice. Her two hundred or so pounds rounded a frame of only a little more than five feet. People who gave the matter any thought assumed 'Sam' was short for 'Samantha,' but no one addressed her by the longer name.

'We had a big crowd for a Sunday night.' Sam maneuvered around the bar and spoke to the only other person in the Red Eye Saloon. 'Guess it was all that excitement at the church this mornin'. Everyone wanted to jaw 'bout it. You were there, weren't you, Leo?'

'Yep.' Leo gazed longingly at the bottles lined up like parading soldiers on the back shelf. Those bottles were out of his reach in every respect. Leo had no money in his pockets and he had already drunk his day's share of the free booze he received as part of his salary for being the Red Eye's swamper.

'You figger goin' to church will git you past the pearly gates? I wonder how many drunks stumble into heaven?'

Leo said nothing. Sam didn't mean to insult him. That was just her way. The saloon owner laughed hard at her own joke as she accompanied the swamper to the front doors of the Red Eye.

'See you tomorra, Leo.' Sam closed the door in front of the bat wings and locked it, leaving the swamper alone on the deserted boardwalk.

As he meandered into the ally between the Red Eye and Franklin's Hardware, Leo wondered if Sam and the bar-keep knew he slept behind the saloon every night. The question evoked a sad laugh. 'Maybe they do, maybe not… guess they don't really care.'

As he reached the back, the swamper saw a large bulge covering part of the ground. The bulge elevated slightly, 'That you, Leo?'

In the moonlight, Leo could see a rubbery, unshaven face looking up at him. 'Yep, Gerald, it's me, hope I didn't wake ya up.'

'Naa, I was jus' restin' my weary bones. Make yourself comfy, I always like to share space with another Confederate.'

'Damn Gerald, can't ya forget the war? It's been over for a dozen years, maybe more. What year is it?'

'I dunno, what difference does it make?'

An uneasy silence followed. Gerald felt bad about angering Leo, who was the closest thing he had to a friend. He decided to change the subject. 'Have ya talked to the marshal 'bout Akando theatenin' to have that Coyote creature kill ya?'

When he answered, Leo tried to sound calm. Gerald scared easily and talked a lot. 'Naa, what's the...'

A dragging sound could be heard coming down the alley. Gerald pushed himself upright as if trying to hear better: 'Sounds like we're havin' company tonight.'

Leo's voice wavered, and it wasn't from drink. 'Guess so...must be Ronnie, didn't he hurt his leg a few days ago?'

'Yep, he limps some, but only some, not...'

The dragging sound got closer. A dark figure rounded the corner and stood still. Leo began to shake as he looked at the newcomer. 'Who are you?'

A low growl came from the figure. Gerald began a fearful moan. 'I don't think that...thing...has a face! What are ya, anyway?!'

The figure lunged toward Leo, who stumbled as he tried to run. Leo was pushed against the back of the saloon, where he gave a horrifying screech of pain.

Gerald saw a rainstorm of blood begin to soak the ground. He cupped his hands over his ears to muffle Leo's cries, and folded into a fetal position.

13

CHAPTER THREE

Stacey Hooper walked down the main street of Conrad, Texas, privately musing over how much smarter he was than anyone else. It was a notion he frequently entertained.

Most gamblers favored the big cities and Stacey spent a fair amount of time in Denver, Dallas and similar locales. 'But, ah, the charm of a Western small town,' he spoke quietly before inhaling on his cigar and sending smoke into the moonlight.

Hooper chortled as he continued his private philosophizing. Small towns furnished little in the way of amusement, and men desperate for diversion could easily be separated from their money. And most gamblers avoided churches. What a mistake. Churches were important gathering points in the West, and much could be learned there even if one did doze during the sermon.

Stacey looked a few doors down at the Red Eye saloon, which had been his first stop that evening. The place was now closed. 'A sure sign my night's work is finished. Time for…'

Frantic voices sounded from the direction of the saloon. Stacey gave a lopsided smile and whispered, 'Aha, the evils of demon drink.'

The voices stopped followed by sharp, desperate cries of pain. An eerie silence followed. Stacey palmed his gun and quietly made his way to the back of the Red Eye. He stopped at the corner and peered around. Two figures lay on the ground.

Stacey ran to the shaking body that moaned in a high-pitched manner like a wounded dog. He crouched over the man while holding on to his gun and inspecting the surroundings. 'What happened here?'

'You were there this mornin', you heard Akando…'

'Yes, you sat beside Leo, your name is Gerald…'

'He tole the truth, Akando did, it really happened, I saw it…'

'What do you mean?'

'Coyote, he killed Leo, it weren't no…'

Gerald choked off his words as footsteps pounded toward them from the alley. 'He's comin' back, Coyote, he's…'

'Hooper, put away that gun! What's going on?' Shem Carson's loud shouts calmed Gerald a bit, and Stacey obeyed the lawman's command as he explained what had brought him to the back of the saloon.

Carson hurried to Leo's body, which now lay face down. He stooped over and held Leo's wrist for a moment, not surprised to feel no pulse.

The marshal sighed as he looked at the woods facing the back of the saloon, on the other side of the narrow dirt road. 'Be easy for whoever did this to vanish into them trees and bushes. It's too dark to pick up a trail… 'sides, the ground there is pretty rocky.'

'Ya ain't dealin' with no human, Marshal! Leo was killed by a monster, by Coyote!'

15

Shem Carson realized he was dealing with a terrified man, and, he thought to himself, a terrified drunk at that. He kept his voice a low monotone as he once again stood over Gerald who remained shaking on the ground. 'Now, I want you to tell me ever'thing that happened here tonight. Take your time and be calm. No one's gonna hurt you.'

'Coyote, he came walkin' slow like, then he attacked Leo fast...like a wolf...'

Gerald remained on the ground as he spoke, as if the dirt provided safety. Shem and Stacey looked down at him and listened patiently, their faces reflecting doubt and frustration as it became obvious that Gerald had little to offer in the way of solid information.

'OK.' Carson offered a hand and pulled the frightened man to his feet. 'Let me know if later on you remember anything about tonight.'

The lawman once again stepped over to the corpse. Reluctantly, as if acting against his better judgement, he turned the body over on its back. 'My God!'

Stacey Hooper also looked down at the victim. His mouth twisted. He said nothing.

Gerald gave a loud scream as he pointed at the horror that lay at their feet. 'No man could do that. That's the work of a monster...of Coyote!'

CHAPTER FOUR

Deputy Rip Gowdy was late in doing his first round. He had arrived at the marshal's office where Shem Carson had told him what had happened to Leo. Carson and he had then been busy talking with the fathers of the schoolchildren and setting up a schedule so the school would be guarded at all times. Akando's threats needed to be taken seriously. Reverend Nate was keeping watch for the morning.

'I'll bet he's havin' a good time,' Gowdy said to himself. 'I've seen the way he looks at Angie Knowland. Imagine, a redskin...'

'Rip Gowdy! On your way to lick the marshal's boots!?'

The words sounded like they came from a barfly. Rip was surprised when he stopped, turned, and saw Howard Dixon yelling at him from the front of the Lucky Ace Saloon. Howard was flanked by three other men. All of them could be called solid citizens. All of them had been in church the previous morning. Now they were standing outside a saloon, looking angry and spoiling for a fight.

Gowdy decided to treat the insult as a joke. He smiled broadly and ambled toward the four men. 'Good to see you gents!'

The men left the boardwalk and made their way into the street to meet the deputy. They stopped a few feet beyond the horses that were tied to a hitch rail. 'We ain't so happy to see you, Deputy. How come you and that marshal won't send them Injun kids on their way? You're settin' up ever'one in this town to be slaughtered by a bunch of savages!'

'This town has law, Howard,' Gowdy replied. 'We're not lettin' some renegade boss us around.'

As Rip spoke, Howard remained in place, but his three companions formed a circle around the deputy. Gowdy heard a familiar voice from behind him. It belonged to George Briggs, the town's barber. 'Well, I've got a gun on you right now, Rip. Maybe the marshal will close the door to a few red-skinned kids for the safe return of his deputy.'

Gowdy silently cursed himself for being so careless. Yes, he was dealing with so-called respectable citizens. But these were also men driven half insane with fear. A fear stoked by alcohol. He should have had his guard up and never allowed them to trap him like this.

The deputy spoke in a low monotone. He didn't want to inflame emotions any higher. 'You men are too smart to be actin' like this. Now…'

'You're the fool, Rip Gowdy!' The voice from behind him grew louder. 'You and that worthless marshal. We know 'bout Leo bein' killed by Coyote. You could end it all right now, but you ain't!'

Howard Dixon smiled, but his face held terror. 'We're takin' you into the Lucky Ace. I got an empty closet you can fill for a while, Deputy.'

Rip Gowdy stood, overwhelmed by his predicament. He was being taken prisoner, in broad daylight, by a group of men who had never broken a law before in their lives. The town of Conrad was close to exploding. If he started a fight and seriously hurt one of his captors, mayhem could break out and the good citizens of Conrad might kill each other before Coyote got another chance.

*

Rance Dehner was looking forward to a few days of rest. He and Stacey Hooper hadn't gone fishing together in over a year: time to do something about that.

Rance reflected on his odd friendship with the gambler. His employer, Bertram Lowrie, founder of the Lowrie Detective Agency, would have conflicting ideas about Stacey Hooper. Gambling was not high on Mr Lowrie's list of approved professions. But his boss knew the value of good connections for a detective, and those connections often involved folks who wouldn't be invited to a governor's ball. Besides, a bullet from Stacey Hooper's gun had saved Dehner's life on more than one occasion, and Rance had repaid the favor many times over. Such incidents were firm footing for a friendship.

As Rance rode into Conrad, where he was to meet Stacey, he saw a man with a badge on his vest surrounded by four townsmen. One of them was holding a gun on the lawman. A small number of people were scattered over the town's boardwalks, watching intently but doing nothing.

'This town has gone crazy,' Dehner whispered to himself.

The detective spurred his horse into a canter toward the four men who were taking Rip Gowdy captive. All four townsmen looked at the intruder and froze with indecision. Dehner leapt on to the gunman. The two men hit the ground. Dehner grabbed the Colt from the squat, moon-faced man and jumped back on to his feet.

Rance knew nothing about the situation, but handed the gun to the lawman, whom he noted was young, with brown freckles and matching hair. 'I hope I just interrupted an elaborate joke.'

'Nothing funny about this, mister.' Gowdy's eyes scanned his four would-be captors. 'Just four gents acting stupid. Very stupid.'

The four townsmen refused to look Gowdy in the eye. The deputy barked angrily at them as he returned the gun. 'Get back to your businesses, all of ya, and don't pull nothin' like this again. Next time, I ain't gonna be so charitable.'

After watching the four men meander off, Dehner introduced himself to the deputy, who responded in kind and then thanked the newcomer. 'Things is gettin' pretty strange 'round here.'

A voice sounded behind the detective. 'Indeed they are, Rip!'

Dehner immediately recognized the voice. He turned, and gave a two-fingered salute to his friend. 'How long have you been in Conrad, Stacey?'

'Long enough to become involved in the civic responsibilities of this thriving town. Come, good friend, we can enjoy some refreshment while I bring you up to date on recent events.'

Despite Stacey's relentless cheerfulness, Rance Dehner felt tense. His thoughts of pleasant days spent fishing began to fade.

CHAPTER FIVE

'Destiny has brought you to this troubled town, good friend,' Stacey declared.

'I thought destiny planned for us to go fishing,' Dehner replied as he tied his horse to a hitch rail and the two men began to make their way down a boardwalk.

The gambler's voice remained buoyant. 'That will come, but first we must rescue a people in dire distress.'

'What's in it for you, Stacey?'

'Why, Rance, surely you know me well enough by now to understand that filthy lucre never motivates my actions.' The gambler slowed his steps and thrust an index finger into the air. 'I suspect you had little more than coffee for breakfast.'

'Well, I knew I'd be in town soon...'

'Of course, that's why you must be my guest!'

Stacey guided his friend into the Red Eye. Rance noted that the establishment looked typical for a Western saloon at mid-morning. There was a scattering of customers, mostly men whose lives had been reduced to drinking and staring at not much of anything. The bartender was preoccupied with setting up for the busy part of the day, and some of his handiwork was apparent – a fresh shine covered the long mahogany bar.

A curious couple had their elbows on that shine. The woman was short and overweight. The man was tall and wiry with blond hair topping the face of a scholar.

'We're in luck, Rance!' Stacey declared. 'I have the honour of introducing you to two of Conrad's finest citizens. The owner of this outstanding establishment, Miss Sam…ah…'

'Sam is enough, Stacey, and forget about the Miss, I ain't no schoolmarm.' Cigarette smoke discharged from Sam's nose and dribbled over her mouth as she spoke.

Stacey continued in his cheerful voice. 'And the gentleman is Jeremy Wilcox, the owner, editor and sole reporter for the *Conrad Gazette.*' He pointed at his companion, 'My good friend, just arrived in town, is Rance Dehner: a detective with the Lowrie Detective Agency in Dallas.'

Wilcox's eyes widened. 'A detective! I was just interviewing Sam about all that went on last night!' He held up a pencil and small notebook as if proving his point.

'I'm not here for…' Rance started to explain.

Stacey interrupted: 'Sam, I know it is a bit late, but are you still serving breakfast?'

The woman took another drag on her cigarette. 'Sure. Satisfying the appetites of men is how I stay in business.' She turned toward the barkeep. 'Tell Earl to fix up some steak and eggs.'

'Make that four servings, I insist on buying breakfast for all of us. And Sam, please set us up with some coffee to start with.'

Dehner was feeling increasingly uneasy. Stacey Hooper had a natural gift for sticking other people with the bill. His sudden generosity was cause for concern. But the detective maintained a friendly smile as the foursome sat down at a round table near the bar. The bartender hastily carried over four cups of coffee on a small platter and placed them down without spilling a drop. He then placed a bowl of sugar and a small container of cream in the middle of the table.

'Thanks, Harry.' His boss's words had a sound of dismissal. Harry made a hasty retreat.

Stacey Hooper sipped his coffee and complimented Sam on her saloon's java before turning to the reporter. 'Jeremy, could you bring Rance up on what has been happening in this town? I know he's very interested.'

Jeremy began with the incident at the church, including the fact that Reverend Nate was an Indian, and continued through the murder of Leo. Hooper's face became unaccustomedly grim as he related his experience in finding Leo's corpse and trying to talk with the terrified Gerald.

Dehner had to acknowledge his friend was right. He did find the events to be interesting. He mulled over what he had just learned as Harry delivered plates of food.

The detective spoke to Jeremy as everyone cut into their steaks. 'From what you say, the Indians who invaded the church yesterday were all carrying new rifles.'

'Yes,' Jeremy confirmed, 'Winchesters.'

'Have there been any reports lately of a large number of Winchesters being stolen?'

'I asked Marshal Carson the same question, Rance. He hasn't heard a peep about rifles of any kind being stolen.'

Dehner paused, allowing the reporter to take a few bites of food before hitting him with another question.

'A school that teaches both Indian children and the children of townspeople and ranchers…is that common?'

'I don't think so,' the reporter chewed on a piece of meat, swallowed and then continued. 'Most reservations are located too far away from towns to make that possible. That's not the case here, but the success of the school goes far beyond a matter of location.'

Dehner noticed a cynical smirk on Sam's face but continued to question the reporter, who seemed anxious to talk. 'What does account for the school's success?'

'Miss Angie Knowland!' Wilcox declared. 'She arrived in Conrad about three years ago with her father, who purchased the general store.'

'And she became the schoolmarm?' Dehner asked.

Jeremy's reply was prim. 'I would rather refer to her as a schoolteacher.'

'OK…she became the schoolteacher?'

'Yes, and as fate would have it, that is when the mission agency that ran the Indian School on the reservation came up with the idea of combining the school with the town's school.'

'And Miss Knowland helped with the transition?'

'She did far more than that!' Jeremy took a bite of egg as he continued to speak. 'Angie Knowland is very well informed. She knew the failings of some of the mission schools and avoided their mistakes. She did not require the Indian children to dress like the children from the town. She encouraged the young people to talk in class about the different ways they lived. She wants her students to learn from each other as well as her.'

Rance smiled his approval. 'Miss Knowland sounds very impressive.'

'Indeed,' Jeremy agreed. 'I've tried to do an article about her but she refuses.' The reporter's voice dropped lower as if partially talking to himself. 'A shame really, I'm sure I could sell a story about Angie and the school to one of the big eastern newspapers.'

Sam waved her smoke in Jeremy's direction, scattering ashes on his coat. 'And how 'bout the *Dallas Chronicle*? Do you think that paper your rich daddy owns would be interested in printin' your story?'

Jeremy's face became red and sullen as he brushed off the ashes. 'My father cares nothing about good journalism.'

Dehner had long ago realized that an important aspect of detective work was asking obvious questions. 'If your father isn't interested in journalism, why does he own a newspaper?'

'To control me, and force me to live the kind of life he does!'

'Could you fill in a few more details?' Dehner asked

'I never knew my mother. She died when I was an infant. My father is a railroad baron who expects me to follow in his footsteps. He was outraged when I took a job at the *Dallas Chronicle*. So he acted like he always does. He bought the *Chronicle* and had me fired.'

Stacey pulled a cigar from his inside coat pocket and spoke before biting off the end. 'And now in the great American tradition of rebellious sons, you have settled in the West and started your own newspaper to prove your father wrong.'

Jeremy nodded his head as if reluctantly acknowledging the gambler was right. 'OK, the *Conrad Gazette* only publishes twice a week. But Conrad is growing and the *Gazette* is growing with it. I use the finest press available, and all of my tools are first rate.'

'Have you thought about doing an article on Reverend Nate?' Dehner asked. 'He sounds like someone with an interesting story.'

Wilcox gave a long sigh. 'I've tried. He hasn't exactly said no, but he keeps putting me off.'

Rance shifted his gaze to the saloon owner. 'What do your customers think of Reverend Nate?'

Sam took a final drag on her cigarette, dropped the stub to the floor and crushed it with her foot. 'There are some folks in this town who think the Injun is wonderful. They seem to think he's the greatest thing to come along since the guy who walked on water.'

Sam needed prodding to continue. Dehner prodded. 'But not everyone thinks that way?'

The woman picked up her steak by the bone and began to chomp on it. She drowned the contents of her mouth in coffee and swallowed before answering the question. 'Nate Enders is an Injun, but he got hisself an education in the East. He don't go round actin' important, but some people are kinda funny 'bout stuff like that.'

'What do you mean?' Dehner asked.

'Ever' night in this saloon I can hear men talkin' 'bout how book learnin' don't count for nothin'. But those same men seem to resent Reverend Nate's fancy talk and the way he can repeat stuff that's in books.'

Dehner smiled good-naturedly. 'What do you think of Reverend Nate, Sam?'

The woman shrugged her shoulders. 'He don't bother me none. Doesn't storm in here spoutin' off 'bout sin. In a way he's kinda like Marshal Shem Carson.'

'I don't follow you,' Dehner said.

'Well...both men are good at their jobs, but they're realistic too. They know that men are men, and gals gotta make a livin'.' The woman's eyes drifted up to the second floor of the saloon where gals made a living.

'Did you sleep in the Red Eye last night?'

'I sleep here ever' night. Some of our customers get rough. I gotta hardcase, Lafe, who takes care of the troublemakers, but he sometimes needs help. I keep a gun by my bedside.'

'Was Lafe on duty last night?'

'Naa. Sunday is his night off. We don't have many stayovers on Sunday night.'

'What about last night?'

'None. The girls slept in a room I keep for 'em at the hotel. They don't like to sleep here when they're not workin'.'

That piece of information impressed the detective as being interesting, but he didn't pursue it. He needed to keep the questions close to the murder. 'Did anything wake you up last night?'

'Sure. I woke up when that poor old sot screamed his head off while getting' sliced up.'

'What did you do?'

The woman gave a slight, mirthless laugh. 'Mr Detective, drunks sleep in back of the Red Eye ever' night. They git in fights, they yell curses at each other, they cry out for their mommies. Last night, I did what I always do. I woke up, patted the Colt on my bedside table, and went back to sleep.'

The woman fumbled in her dress pocket for a tobacco pouch and papers. 'Yep, I sleep with that gun ever' night and it makes me feel more comfy than any man ever did.'

This time her laugh was loud and bitter.

*

He watched from a remote corner table of the Red Eye. The glass in front of him had been empty for some time. He was confident no one was watching him. No one pays attention to a man drinking alone in the morning hours.

After the group at the table near the bar had departed, the man arose from the dense circle of smoke surrounding him and made his way to the bar. 'Gettin' ready for a busy day, Harry?'

Harry had been stocking the shelves behind the bar. He turned his head and at first the look on his face was suspicious. At this hour, a lot of the customers were hopeless drunks who pleaded for just one free drink. But the suspicion dissipated. Harry didn't know the speaker's name, but he recognized a customer who always paid.

'Yep,' Harry resumed his work on the shelves, 'gotta lot to do.' He hoped the customer would take the hint.

That didn't happen. 'Say, one of those guys jawin' with Sam, was his name Rance Dehner?'

This time Harry didn't turn around to answer. 'Yeh, think that was his name.'

'Know how long he's gonna be in town?'

'For a spell. From what I could hear he's gettin' involved in stoppin' all this Coyote business.'

The man left without saying any more. A few minutes later, Harry forgot he had even spoken with him.

CHAPTER SIX

'As usual you are right, my friend,' Stacey Hooper beamed a smile as he spoke. 'We need to speak with Sahale. This threat from Akando needs to be resolved quickly, and you are just the man for the job.'

After finishing their breakfast, Rance had suggested to Stacey that they ride out to the reservation to get some background information from the Wichita Chief, Sahale. There really wasn't much else they could do at the time. Conrad's two lawmen were busy. Reverend Nate and Angie Knowland were occupied at the school.

Dehner was sure Stacey had a reason for stopping Akando that was less than altruistic. He had decided to stop pressing his friend on the matter. The truth would eventually emerge.

'I have met Sahale before,' Hooper continued. 'He's in town occasionally to...' The gambler noticed the squint in Dehner's eyes. 'See something?'

Rance nodded toward a hill on their left. 'A moment ago there was one Indian at the top of that hill, now there are three.'

Hooper glanced leftward. 'Now three more are joining them. This doesn't have the look of a late morning tea.'

As if to prove Stacey's point, a loud war whoop cut the air, followed by the pounding of hooves as half a dozen Indians rode downward toward the trail, firing rifles. Dehner and Hooper spurred their horses into a fast run.

Dehner's bay spread its body out as its legs extended to their full reach, appearing to almost consume the ground. But the detective knew his steed couldn't maintain the pace. The animal had already been ridden hard that day.

Rance shouted at his friend whose claybank was almost even with him. 'Know if there's any place close we can take cover?'

'Alas, professional responsibilities have kept me in town. I'm not familiar with the geography.'

Dehner pointed to his right. 'That boulder up ahead… it'll have to do.'

The rifle shots grew closer as Dehner and Hooper reined in behind the boulder and ground tethered their horses. They pulled rifles from their saddle boots and took refuge behind the large stone, which stood at about seven feet.

The Indians kept coming at them, now moving faster on the flat ground of the trail. Dehner quickly pivoted beside the boulder and fired his Winchester. The body of the Indian closest to them jerked backwards, his weapon dropped to the ground and he plunged from his horse. His body writhed in the dust before going limp.

The remaining five Indians rode up a large hill on the opposite side of the trail from the boulder. Except for small stones and scraggly brush the hill stood desolate.

'Our adversaries are without cover,' Stacey said.

'Yes, but they're up pretty high on that hill. Our chances of hitting them are not good.'

Hooper remained cheerful. 'But they can't shoot us either. For the time being, we're safe.'

Dehner laughed caustically. 'For a gambler you have your odds all wrong.'

'What do you mean?'

As if in answer to Stacey's question two Indians rode swiftly down the hill and began shooting at their enemies. Dehner and Hooper returned fire. The two Indians rode back to the top of the hill.

'The opposition is obviously desperate,' Stacey proclaimed. 'That little scrap they initiated was downright pathetic. We made them run like rabbits.'

'And we used up ammunition in the process.' Dehner sounded grave.

'So did they!'

'They have five rifles, we have two, who do you think will run out of ammunition first? They'll keep on riding down, firing and forcing us to use up ammunition to hold them back until we have nothing left to throw at them.'

'That will take a while, but…' Stacey's face turned grim. 'It seems that all those stories about Indians being remarkably patient are true.'

Two different Indians began a fast ride downward toward their targets. 'Don't fire yet,' As he spoke Dehner spotted some motion on the far right of the hill. He touched Hooper on the shoulder and pointed upwards. 'I don't know if this is good news or not.'

A figure who was at first only a shadow against the bright sun rode toward the two attacking Indians. He fired a rifle in the air, obviously a warning shot.

'That's Sahale!' Hooper exclaimed.

One of the Indians heeded the warning. He turned his horse and galloped up the hill.

The second attacker looked with awe at the oncoming chief, but only for a moment. He quickly dismounted, hoping solid ground would assure accuracy, and aimed his rifle at Sahale.

The chief continued to ride directly at the man who wanted to kill him. The boldness was justified. The Indian who was now on foot missed on his first attempt and began to frantically lever the Winchester. He couldn't move fast enough. Sahale, still on horseback, raised his rifle and brought his opponent down with one shot.

The remaining four Indians at the top of the hill galloped off as Sahale dismounted and crouched over the man he had just killed. The chief slowly stood and walked toward Hooper and Dehner who were walking toward him.

'Sahale, we were just coming to visit you,' the gambler's voice was effusive. 'I'm so glad you dropped in on us at a time when we were in dire need of assistance.'

'Stacey, you have been given a gift for creating laughter when there is little cause for joy. That is a great gift.'

Dehner was a bit surprised by the chief's good English. As Stacey introduced the two men and they shook hands Rance noticed that while Sahale stood at less than average height he had a firm, muscular build. The black hair that was banded and flowed over his shoulders was only lightly infused with gray. Dehner reckoned the chief to be in his early forties.

Sahale looked back at the man he had just killed. He said nothing and Dehner sensed an intensity in the chief's silence. The Indian's eyes then shifted to the body lying on the trail.

'I'm afraid that is my work, Chief Sahale,' Dehner said.

The chief smiled at his new acquaintance. 'Please call me Sahale, and I will call you Rance.'

'Did Akando lead this attack, Sahale?' Dehner asked.

'Yes. I spotted Akando on the taller hill behind this one. He was watching the battle like a chief. Your attackers were young braves who wanted to impress Akando.' The Indian paused, as if wondering whether to continue with his thoughts, then apparently decided it was worth the effort. 'Marshal Shem Carson calls these renegades "outlaws", and in many ways he is right. Shem Carson is a good man, but he doesn't completely understand that these are hard days for Indians.'

Stacey's face crunched up. 'Why? The serious fighting is over.'

'That's my point,' Sahale answered. 'The great warriors are gone. Crazy Horse is dead. Sitting Bull is in Canada. According to the *Conrad Gazette* he's asking the government up there for a reserve.'

Hooper appeared amused by the Indian's statement. 'Do you read newspapers?'

Sahale nodded his head. 'Smoke signals work well in giving out certain information, but their use is very limited.'

The three men shared a laugh before Sahale continued in a wistful voice. 'Many of our young men are restless and angry, though they do not know why. Such men are easy prey for dangerous fools like Akando. They were in this area today trying to harm me.'

Both Rance and Stacey gave their companion questioning stares. He answered their unstated question. 'I capture wild horses and sell them. They were seeking the horses before I found them in order to kill them. They have done such needless killing before.'

Dehner's face still had a questioning look. 'Why did they attack us?'

'I'm certain they wanted to kill Stacey.'

Hooper's eyebrows shot up. 'Why?!'

'You were at the church last Sunday when Akando threatened Nata...I mean Nate.' Sahale said. 'From what I have been told, you managed to anger Akando, I don't know how.'

Hooper once again looked amused. 'That's another one of my gifts, making people angry.'

Dehner moved matters in a different direction. 'We were coming to ask you about Akando. Why would he demand that Indian children be kept away from school?'

'School is a very hard matter for our tribe,' the chief answered. 'About half of our children go to school. The other half have families who keep them away.'

'Why?' Dehner asked.

'Many of the Wichita fear that children will use what they learn in school to become part of the white man's world. Already, some of our people have left the tribe to take jobs on ranches. A few have even gone to places like Dallas in hope of finding great wealth.'

'I understand,' Dehner replied, 'but...'

'Akando is a man who seeks attention and glory,' Sahale continued. 'And like many such men he is without careful thoughts. Akando does not make plans. Someone is making plans for him.'

Sahale turned his head to gaze at the two corpses. 'I must get these men back to their families.'

Dehner and Hooper helped the chief wrap the corpses in blankets and get them on to their horses, which had been drinking at a small stream nearby. At first the horses were made nervous by the smell of blood, but they quickly calmed down.

Sahale mounted his own steed and held a rope that was tied to the reins of the horses with their gruesome cargo. He thanked Rance and Stacey for their help.

Dehner nodded at the chief, and asked what he intended to be a casual question: 'Do you allow your own children to attend school?'

'My wife and children died years ago from a white man's disease.'

'I'm sorry,' Dehner said.

'The doctor in Conrad offered to come out and care for them. I would not let him. Akando is not the only dangerous fool.'

Dehner said quietly to Stacey as he watched the chief ride off: 'A lonely, tortured man carrying two dead bodies back to their families.'

CHAPTER SEVEN

Deputy Rip Gowdy looked at the eleven Indian children, all of whom were now mounted on their ponies in front of the school house. They looked comfortable on their mounts. *Hell, those kids must learn to ride about the time they stop crawling.*

Gowdy had to admit he enjoyed being around the kids, and was even looking forward to seeing they got safely back to the reservation. 'OK, ever'body ready to move?'

The children all responded with smiles. They seemed excited about being accompanied by a man wearing a badge. *That's sure an improvement over how some of the town folks have been acting lately.*

Gowdy and his charges waved to Reverend Nate, Angie Knowland and the two remaining children who were still at the school as they rode off. As the group got further into the distance Angie addressed the boy and girl standing beside her: they were nine and eight respectively.

'Adam, Esther, you're sure your father said he'd be coming for you?'

'Yes ma'am,' Adam answered.

Reverend Nate smiled at the two youngsters. 'Until your father gets here I want the two of you to help me with my history. Now, the first President of the United States was… ah…Davy Crockett!'

As the playfulness between the pastor and the children continued, Angie Knowland watched in admiration. Nate Enders fitted no one's idea of a preacher. He stood well over six feet with a muscular build made to look even more powerful by his copper skin. His hair was the color of coal and carefully groomed in the style of a bank manager.

As she saw Pete Clement coming in a buckboard to pick up Adam and Esther, she hoped Reverend Enders would volunteer to ride with her as she returned home. She conceded to herself that the notion was ridiculous. Home for Angie Knowland was Knowland's General Store, less than a twenty-minute ride away. Still, she thought, Nate Enders did, at times, seem to look at her in a certain way…

The woman quickly vanquished such thoughts from her mind, or tried to…she should be ashamed of herself. She and the pastor could never…

'Sorry I'm late, hope my varmints ain't been too much trouble!' Pete Clements yelled. The woman, lost in her thoughts, had shoved the oncoming wagon to the back of her mind. 'Ah…hello…ah…they've been no trouble at all.'

The two children told Pete about the fun they had been having with Reverend Nate as they tied their pony, which they had ridden to school, to the back of the wagon and climbed aboard. Pete's voice lost its joviality as he looked at the preacher. 'How did things go today, Reverent? Did all your volunteers show up like they said?'

'There were no problems. I was here all day. Rip Gowdy is riding with the Indian children, and Brad Taylor, little Maddie Taylor's father, is with the other kids as they ride home.'

Pete smiled, revealing a mouth with several missing teeth. 'I got me some stuff to do in town today. Figgered I could pick up these two varmints, seein' how I live a bit further out than most.' He waved good-bye, as did the two children while the buckboard pulled away.

After they finished returning the waves, Reverend Nate and Angie both looked at the ground, then they looked back at the school house and then they looked at each other.

'Miss Knowland, please allow me to ride with you back to your home.'

Miss Knowland made a few token statements about the pastor's offer being unnecessary before politely giving in. The couple untied the horses from the rack in front of the school and began to ride.

'I'm sorry you had to spend the whole day at the school, Reverend Enders, I know how busy you are.'

'Please call me Reverend Nate, or just Nate – everyone does. And may I call you Angie?'

Angie sensed she was blushing and glanced away before answering. 'Yes, of course, Reverend Enders – I mean, Reverend Nate.'

Angie's correction allowed the couple a chance to release some nervousness through laughter. But the laughter went on too long and was followed by a nervous silence. Angie spoke into it. 'October first is next Monday. Why do you think Akando has given us a week to decide whether or not to allow Indian children to attend school?'

Nate had been hoping for a lighter subject, but grabbed at whatever the teacher offered. 'Akando wants to be feared. I'm afraid we are in for a difficult week. Akando wants the citizens of Conrad to be shaking in their shoes because of him.'

'From what I can tell, he has already succeeded in that regard.'

The pastor nodded in agreement and paused before speaking in a less grim manner. 'The school year is certainly getting off to a rough start, Angie. After this, putting up with mischievous children will seem an easy task.'

Reverend Nate had hoped his words would brighten the young woman's mood. That didn't happen. Angie continued to look troubled. 'I won't have to worry about mischievous children much longer. This will be my last year teaching.'

'Why's that?'

'You've been reading the bulletins from the mission agency,' she answered. 'They want qualified teachers in all their schools. I hardly fit the bill. My education stopped at the eighth grade.'

They were now entering the town's busiest area, consisting of shops and saloons. Nate Enders noted that a fair number of people were looking at him and Angie. Many of them smiled and waved but there were those who looked on with strong disapproval or something worse.

Nate forgot about the onlookers and focused on what he had just been told. 'The mission agency is staffed by very realistic people who understand the west. Yes, in their formal writings, they want teachers with a college education, but you are well read and able to convey knowledge...'

'The children of this town and the reservation deserve the best, and I am not able to give it to them.'

'Angie, you are a wonderful teacher, and I so much appreciate...'

A loud laugh silenced the pastor. Dade Knowland stepped out of the front door of Knowland's General Store and followed his laugh with a good-natured shout. 'Looks like you two survived the school day!'

Reverend Nate tried to say something that matched Dade's good humour as he watched Angie give her father a fragile smile. The young woman dismounted and tied up her horse at the hitch rail that fronted the store.

Dade Knowland was a big man with wide shoulders, a round face and huge arms. He had become a widower after only a few years of marriage, and from what Nate could ascertain, had worked hard to provide a good life for his daughter.

Angie embraced her father as she spoke. 'I'm going to get busy with preparing tomorrow's lessons. I'll attend to my horse later.' She hurried into the store.

Dade remained on the boardwalk. 'Everything go OK today, Preacher?'

'Sure did, Dade!' Nate nodded a friendly goodbye and rode off.

Dade watched the pastor slowly fade into the distance. 'You're lyin', preacher,' he whispered to himself. 'I seen how my daughter looked just now.'

Dade Knowland had been carefully watching how Reverend Nate and his daughter behaved around each other for several months. He continued to whisper. 'Angie is startin' to really care fer that guy, and it's hurtin' her awful. I gotta do somethin' quick. But what?'

CHAPTER EIGHT

Pete Clement halted his buckboard at the edge of town. Knowland's General Store stood at the opposite end of the street. His face took on a mischievous glow as he handed coins to his two children.

'Your Daddy's got himself some business to do. While I'm takin' care of the borin' stuff, you two can go to the store and fetch some candy.'

Adam and Esther squealed their excitement. Pete lifted his index finger indicating there was more good news to come. 'And whilst you eat your candy you can have a look-see at the dime novels Mr Knowland's got in his store. Pick out one you want and I'll pay for it when I come for you.'

The children shouted thank you as they jumped off the wagon and began to run down the boardwalk. Pete watched them with a sense of wonderment. They were such fine kids and he would do whatever it took to give them and their mother a good home. He glanced behind for a moment at the cargo on the flat bed of the wagon. The gesture seemed to bring him back down to earth. Yes, he would do what it took.

He guided the buckboard down a narrow road that could barely contain the wagon and stopped at the back entrance of the Red Eye Saloon. He sat immobile for a moment recalling that a murder had taken place on this spot the previous night. Without exactly intending to, his eyes examined the ground for blood. He silently chastised himself for such foolishness. There was business that needed doing.

He stepped off the wagon and pulled the tarp from the flatbed, exposing a large array of jugs containing moonshine. He moved quickly to the back door, knocked and listened to the heavy footsteps approaching from within.

A monster of a man opened the door. Lafe had been hired by Sam to intimidate people, and when necessary beat them up. The man seemed fit for nothing else. He was huge, with pale skin, a pockmarked face and a receding hairline that pushed almost to the middle of his head. His eyes were flat and angry.

Pete worked hard at sounding cheerful. 'I got the stuff!'

Lafe replied in a low growl. Pete couldn't make out his words, but helped the man carry the jugs into the back room of the saloon.

Pete's first attempt at selling moonshine had been a scary lesson in how business was done in Conrad, Texas. He had been selling jugs from his wagon a short distance outside of town on a Saturday afternoon. The word had spread and he was quickly surrounded by customers. Those customers scattered when Lafe had appeared, riding a grey.

'You're comin' with me,' the huge man said.

'I'm plenty happy right where I am, stranger.'

Pete immediately regretted his bravado. Lafe dismounted, picked Pete up and threw him toward the front of the wagon. 'Ya only git one warnin'. Do what I tell ya.'

Pete did what he was told. Lafe led him to the back of the Red Eye where Sam was waiting. She grabbed one of the jugs off of the wagon, pulled the cork and took a sip.

The saloon owner smiled approvingly at the newcomer. 'You make good tanglefoot, mister. Now, let me explain how we handle moonshine in this here fine town.'

Pete Clement quickly fell in line with the saloon owner's demands. As he placed two jugs on the floor of the storage room he admitted to himself that working for Sam had helped him to...

'Whatcha workin' up a sweat for, Pete?' Sam's voice now sounded less threatening than it had on their first meeting. Pete knew that could change quickly if he crossed her.

Clement smiled at the woman as she entered through the door that connected the storage room to the main floor of the saloon. 'I'm jus' helpin' Lafe unload...'

'Lafe can handle it all by his lonesome, he's hired for his muscle. Let's you and me chew the fat.'

'Sure,' Pete answered nervously, as a black cat which had accompanied Sam scampered by him and ran outside.

Sam laughed and gave her companion a mocking stare. 'You superstitious 'bout black cats?'

Clement's jangled nerves had been caused by Sam, not the cat, but he wasn't about to tell her that. 'Well...sorta... you know my wife Mona, she's real superstitious, guess some of it rubbed off on me.'

'I've heard 'bout that wife of yours, some folks say she gets mighty jumpy on a Friday the thirteenth.'

'Folks is right.' Clement pointed at the black cat which had leaped on to the flatbed of the wagon. 'What's his name?'

'He ain't gotta name,' Sam replied bluntly. 'The cat catches mice. He does his job, that's all that matters to me.'

'Of course…'

For a moment, Sam said nothing as she watched Lafe bring in the last of the jugs. She waved her hand in dismissal and her hired hand departed.

'Things ain't goin' so well on that ten head ranch of yours, are they, Pete?'

'No. Most of my stock died.'

Sam pulled brown papers and a tobacco pouch from a large pocket in her dress and began to build a smoke. 'And the big ranchers won't buy what you got left, they're afraid your cows will infect their herd.'

'Ah… yes.'

'You still got plans for a big ranch someday?'

'Sure do.'

'Ain't that grand!' Sam returned the fixings to her pocket, then ran a tongue across the brown paper and folded it into a cigarette. 'The west is a land of foolish men with foolish dreams. Funny thing 'bout dreams, they get lifted high by booze, then washed away.'

She reached into the same dress pocket and brought out a match. She lighted the match with a thumb nail and put the flame to her cigarette. 'You started making moonshine to help keep your ranch goin'…right?'

'That's right, Sam.'

'Now the tail's waggin' the dog. Moonshine is what's keepin' food on the table.'

Clement nodded his head.

Smoke shot from Sam's nostrils as she looked at the jugs on the floor behind her. 'Some jaspers jus' prefer tangle-foot to the legal stuff, they say it gives 'em more of a kick, and they're willin' to pay for it. Many of 'em drink at the bar for hours, then buy a jug to take home.' She turned to Pete and her voice suddenly became harsh. 'Done much jawin' with Howard Dixon lately?'

'Dixon...the owner of the Lucky Ace...no.'

Sam's voice dropped a bit. She was getting to the point. 'Howard stopped by to see me yesterday. Pretended he was jus' bein' friendly with the competition. Dixon's a smooth talker, he's a lot more high hat than me, I'll give him that.'

A look of resentment creased Sam's face as she continued. 'So, Howard asks me real casual like where I'm gettin' my tanglefoot from. He buys from Charlie Bell, like I used ta. Your stuff is better, and I don't think that slick Howard Dixon even knows you're in the business.'

Pete felt good. He had thought about approaching the owner of the Lucky Ace, but hadn't gotten around to it. Now he could truthfully say, 'Dixon might not even know my name.'

A note of threat came into Sam's voice. 'Keep it that way. In another year or so Dixon will be gone and I'll be owner of the Lucky Ace. That ain't no dream. I'm takin' over the saloon business in this town. It'll take a while, but it's gonna happen. You wanta be on the winnin' side, Pete.'

'Sure, Sam.'

Sam indulged in a few more minutes of blustery talk before dismissing Clement. As Pete returned to his wagon, the black cat jumped off the flatbed and ran in front of him. Clement's body shivered. The animal seemed to be warning him.

CHAPTER NINE

Pete's evening started off good. He ate a delicious supper and played with his children until their bedtime. As Adam and Esther went to their room for a story, Pete left the house to attend to chores. He returned to his house after putting the horses in the barn for the night. Mona was just coming out of the bedroom. She smiled at her husband and waved a dime novel at him.

'*Buffalo Bill Versus the Phantom Bandits,*' she declared in a mock dramatic voice. 'The children sure do love the stories you buy for 'em. I had ta read 'em the whole thing 'fore they would go to sleep. Keep gittin' books for Adam and Esther. They need somethin' special now and agin'.'

'I wish I could buy something special for you, Mona, but right now…'

'Shush!' She hastily walked toward her husband and put two fingers on his lips. 'We knowed we was gonna face some hard times when we came West.'

'Yep, but you didn't know you were gonna be the wife of a moonshiner.'

'That's only for the time bein'…'till we get on our feet.'

Mona was a petite, brown-haired woman with sloping shoulders brought on by heavy work. She placed the book on the only table in the room and smiled at her husband. 'There's still some of that pie left from dinner if ya'd like some.'

'That surely does…'

A loud pounding sound came from outside followed by silence. Pete moved toward the house's front window and opened the shutters. 'Sounded like it came from the barn, but I don't see nothin'.'

The second time, the racket was more of a bang, Pete stuck his head out of the glassless window. 'It's comin' from the barn all right, but I still don't see anythin' unusual.'

'Maybe one of the horses broke outta the stall and is kickin'' – Mona wrung her hands as she spoke.

Pete Clement realized his wife was terrified. 'Yes, I'm sure that's it. I'll go tend to the nag.'

There was another bang. Pete moved to the coat rack, removed a holster and six gun, then strapped it around his waist. 'I'm jus' bein' careful.'

'Pete, don't go!'

Clement placed a hand on his wife's shoulder. 'I gotta. Now, I'll be back in a minute. If 'n I'm not, you know where the Henry is.'

As Pete started for the door his wife grabbed his arm and handed him an object she had hastily removed from around her neck. 'Take this with you.'

Despite the circumstances, Pete had to smile. His wife had handed him a heart-shaped locket. The locket contained her lucky penny, a coin she had found as a child.

He gently placed Mona's penny necklace into his shirt pocket. 'I'll be bringin' it back to you soon.'

Pete stepped out of the house and strode toward the barn. He was pretty sure what was going on. His still was located behind the barn. Howard Dixon might not know who he was, but it was a good bet Charlie Bell knew all about him. He had taken the Red Eye's business away from Bell and several ranchers had been buying direct from Clement, telling him his moonshine topped that of Bell.

'Charlie's probably back there wreckin' my still,' Pete whispered to himself. 'Gotta do somethin' 'bout that.'

But do what? He knew he could never shoot a man for busting up a still. Maybe a warning shot might scare him off. As Clement reached the barn, he drew his gun and began to move toward the back. He paused for a moment at the barn's back edge before almost jumping to where he could see the still. Pete was hoping for the advantage of surprise.

Pete Clement was the surprised one. The still stood untouched. There was no one there.

A loud, shrill laugh blared from the side of the barn. Clutching his pistol a little tighter, Pete turned and stepped back toward the barn's side. He still saw nothing. Suddenly a figure seemed to disconnect from the darkness created by the barn's overhang.

'Wha...'

At first Pete felt nothing except a terrible weakness, then pain seared through his body and he dropped to the ground, his gun making a rattling sound as it hit a stone somewhere beside him. Through blurred vision he saw a knife plunging downward. He tried to do a fast roll to escape the blade, but could only move his head far enough to see Mona's heart shaped locket with the lucky penny lying on the ground beside him.

CHAPTER TEN

Jeremy Wilcox gazed out the window of the small building that housed the *Conrad Gazette*. Adam Clement was riding his pony into town at a fast clip. No one else in town seemed to take notice.

Wilcox took notice. He hurried out of the building, looked down the street and spotted Adam dismounting in front of the marshal's office. The reporter began a brisk walk in that direction. As he drew near, Shem Carson, Stacey Hooper and Rance Dehner came running out with the boy. They all mounted quickly and rode off.

Wilcox stepped into the middle of the street and watched the dust cloud kicked up by the riders. They seemed to be heading for the church.

Jeremy began to mull over the events as he returned to the *Gazette* office. He was certain what had happened. Adam had brought very bad news. Shem Carson and his friends were taking Reverend Nate with them to help out the Clements.

'A good reporter would follow them!' Jeremy said aloud to no one as he entered the office and slammed the door.

When he had worked for the *Dallas Chronicle* people had treated him with respect. No one even thought about telling him he didn't belong at the scene of a crime. They understood the power and influence of the *Chronicle*. And then came that awful day when he was cast out from his job.

Jeremy again spoke aloud. 'The *Gazette* isn't the *Chronicle* and Conrad isn't Dallas.'

The journalist knew that in Conrad the law would try to run him off as being a nuisance. And if the story of his being a pest got around, Dade Knowland and some of the other merchants would pull their advertising from the paper.

He couldn't allow that to happen, it might ruin all of his plans.

Wilcox inhaled deeply. No sense in getting upset, he had always been flexible and there were many ways to handle this situation. He walked over to the small stove in the office and began to make a fresh pot of coffee. This would be a long night.

*

Less than two hours later, Wilcox's speculations proved correct. The reporter was once again staring out the window of the newspaper office, casually watching Rip Gowdy do a round when a buckboard clattered into town. Shem Carson was driving. Mona Clement shared the seat, her two children were in the flatbed. Three men, Rance Dehner, Stacey Hooper, and Reverend Nate were riding behind the wagon, which headed for the marshal's office. Rip Gowdy began to run after the buckboard; so did Jeremy.

The commotion caused a small crowd of late night saloon patrons to gather around the marshal's office to witness the scene as Shem Carson helped Mona and her children off the wagon, while the three horsemen tied up their steeds at the hitch rail. Jeremy got close enough to hear the marshal talking to Mona.

'You jus' need to answer a few questions, Mona. After that, Reverend Nate will take you and the children over to stay with the Staffords.'

The woman stared at the ground and nodded her head.

'What happened, Mona?' The shouted question came from Howard Dixon.

Mona Clement looked up, her face a pale mask of terror. 'Pete is dead!' she screamed. 'It happened like the Indian said last Sunday. He was killed by a monster…Coyote!'

Mona's scream drew loud cries from the onlookers. Jeremy couldn't make out exactly what was being said, but they were angry and scared.

'All of you, git!' Rip Gowdy shouted as the entourage made its way into the marshal's office. 'None of ya got any business here.'

'The law 'round here is lettin' us all get killed and you say it's none of our business – what kinda lawman are ya?' Dixon's question was aimed at Rip Gowdy's back as the deputy hurried inside the office and closed the door.

With no one left to yell at, the onlookers began to speak among themselves in lowered voices. None of them seemed to notice Jeremy Wilcox, and that was fine with the reporter. This was a story he could write up. The news was happening in public, he was a bystander and not interfering with the law. Shem Carson might not like having news of Coyote in the *Gazette* but he wouldn't complain…not openly anyway.

The saloon patrons remained in the street, their voices dropping to whispers. Wilcox stood by totally silent. Another story could be brewing right here.

The group began to break up. Several wandered off, but a tight-knit bunch of six men started to walk in a determined manner toward the Lucky Ace Saloon.

Looks like they have more in mind then a last drink before going home, the reporter mused. He allowed the group to get several steps ahead of him, then followed behind.

Howard led the men through the batwings. The procession marched toward the saloon owner's office, which was located at the back.

Wilcox hurried around to the back. A fragile film of yellow suddenly ignited from the office window. The reporter froze in place as an awkward squeaking noise cut the silence. After lighting a kerosene lamp, Howard was opening the window to help diminish the stifling heat of a hot Texas night.

Jeremy Wilcox crawled under the window and listened.

CHAPTER ELEVEN

Four men eyed Jeremy Wilcox as he stepped into the marshal's office. The reporter mentally assessed each one. Shem Carson and Rip Gowdy looked irritated. They always regarded him as a bother. Rance Dehner looked neutral, while Stacey Hooper appeared amused. But then, life itself seemed to amuse the gambler.

'I have something important to tell you!' the reporter declared dramatically.

'And jus' what might that be?' Gowdy's voice was dismissive.

Jeremy Wilcox smile inwardly. He was about to whittle the deputy down a notch. 'Howard Dixon, George Briggs and four other men are planning to get up a gang of citizens to arm themselves and stand in front of the school house tomorrow morning. They won't allow the Indian children to enter.'

The atmosphere inside the office changed immediately. Wilcox continued to be inwardly amused as Shem Carson sprang from his office chair and urgency filled his voice. 'How do you know this?'

Stacey Hooper spoke up. 'I suspect that Jeremy, in the best tradition of the fourth estate, listened in at the door, or was it the window, while Dixon and the rest of them made their plans.'

'It was the window,' Jeremy said.

'Besides Dixon and Briggs, who else was in on this meeting?' Dehner asked.

'Vince Bursey, who owns the saddle shop, and three others who seemed to be barflies...I don't know their names.'

'But you're sure 'bout their plans?' the marshal asked. 'All six men are gonna be at the school house tomorra mornin' to stop the Indian kids?'

'More than just six men,' Wilcox declared confidently. 'Right now they're spreading out over town – even some of the closer ranches – and waking up people that'll help them. They plan to have a mob on hand to greet the Indian kids.'

Marshal Shem Carson stood silent for a moment, and then quickly glanced at the three men in the office. 'I reckon we better start wakin' up some folks ourselves.'

*

Angie Knowland slowly walked down the aisle of the church, her father at her side. She was wearing a beautiful wedding gown, the one she had seen in the catalogue they had at the store. She had frequently looked at the drawing when she was by herself, embarrassed by her own foolish desires.

But now her wish was coming true. The church was decorated by beautiful flowers and she was walking toward Nate Enders, his face filled with love as he held out his arms to her.

When she arrived at the front of the church, Nate took her hands as he remained on the platform and began to conduct his own wedding ceremony. It should have looked ridiculous, but it didn't – everything looked beautiful and right.

Nate stepped off the platform as he reached the end of the ceremony. 'If anyone here knows why this man and woman should not be bound together in holy matrimony, let him speak up now, or forever hold his peace.'

A terrible pounding sound came from the back of the church. Angie looked around her: the flowers had all died. The pounding became louder, and Nate suddenly disappeared. Her father turned his head away, refusing to look at her.

*

Angie's eyes opened and she glanced at the ceiling of her room as she did at the beginning of every day. But this morning was different. The room was still dark and...

She heard her father opening the front door of the store, and distant voices. 'Reverend Nate, is something wrong?'

'I'm afraid so, can I come in?'

He's here to tell father about my dreams about how I... Angie inhaled and tried to calm herself. *I'm back in the real world.* There seemed to be an emergency. She needed to get moving. She got out of bed, put on a robe and slippers, and paused briefly in front of a mirror before hurrying down to the store from her second-floor bedroom.

Reverend Nate looked both worried and apologetic as he stood in front of the store's counter with her father, who was also in his robe and slippers. 'I'm sorry to wake you up, Angie, but we have a serious problem.'

'What is it, Nate?' As Angie asked the question she noticed the expression on her father's face. He had taken note that his daughter and the preacher were on a first name basis, but Dade Knowland said nothing. This was obviously not the time to be discussing such matters.

Nate quickly summarized the situation involving the mob that was going to block the school house that morning. He had received the information from Rance Dehner.

'So, our so-called good citizens have turned into a gang of thugs that threaten my daughter and a group of children whose sin is that they want to go to school!' Dade almost shouted his words.

'Yes,' Nate replied, 'but we're going to stop them.' He focused his attention on Angie. 'I'm taking you out to the Taylor ranch. Rip Gowdy will be taking the children from the reservation there, and Shem Carson is bringing the rest of the kids. You will keep the children at the ranch until we send a messenger to let you know that the trouble is over, then you can bring them all to the school.'

'Have the Taylors agreed to this?' Angie asked.

Reverend Nate replied with a sheepish grin. 'I think so, Dehner has gone out to the Taylor place to alert them to the emergency. They are good people who believe in the importance of educating kids, and of course their daughter attends the school. I'm sure they'll go along. And the Taylors have plenty of good ranch hands who will make sure no one tries to attack the ranch, and later on will escort you and the children back to the school.'

Dade gave a troubled sigh before speaking. 'Wouldn't it be easier and safer to call off school for the day?'

'That's what I thought at first,' the pastor said. 'But Rance changed my mind. If we give in to a group of scared locals, that will only encourage Akando, who is backed up by a band of warriors.'

Despite the talk of danger, Angie experienced a feeling of intimacy and even comfort. She was standing in a store which she regarded as part of her home with the two most important men in her life: her father and the man she loved. They were discussing a problem they would solve together.

And, yes, she admitted to herself that the very informal attire everyone was wearing increased the feeling of intimacy. She had never seen Reverend Nate dressed in such a way – a red checkered shirt and Levis. A gun, which appeared to be a .44, was strapped to his hip.

'Is that OK, Angie?'

The woman realized she was being addressed. 'Ah… pardon…Nate?'

Reverend Nate repeated his words. 'I'm ready to ride with you out to the Taylor ranch, is that OK, are you willing to go?'

'Yes, yes of course, I'll go change.'

'I'll change too, and I'll be there,' Dade said.

'Be where, Father?'

'The schoolhouse, we're going to stand up to those fools,' Dade smiled in a quizzical manner. 'Haven't you been listening?'

'Oh yes, yes, of course.' She hurried off to get her clothes on.

*

Nate and Angie rode at a gallop, which didn't allow for conversation. As they drew near to the Taylor ranch they could see lights and activity. Two men were standing at the gate of the fence which surrounded the large ranch.

'Sentries have already been posted,' Reverend Nate said as both he and his companion slowed their horses. 'But no children seem to have arrived yet. We're in plenty of time.'

'Be careful, Nate.' The woman pointed in the direction of his gun. 'I guess I'm a bit nervous, I've never seen you armed before.'

'I hope you'll never have to see me armed again.'

They were drawing close to the gate. In a few minutes, Angie knew they would be parting and Nate would return to the school. She looked at the man riding beside her. 'Do you think all this will ever end? Will townspeople and Indians be able to live together in peace?'

Reverend Nate sensed there was a lot behind that question. 'It is up to people like you and me to make sure that day happens…it won't come easily.'

'Mornin' Preacher, Miss Angie.'

'Good morning, Trey,' Nate returned the greeting from a member of his congregation. Trey stood by the gate to the ranch holding a Henry, while his fellow sentry walked the large gate open for Angie.

'You haven't let any grass grow under your feet, Trey.' The pastor was disappointed that his conversation with Angie had to end and tried to cover it with a friendly remark.

'After that Dehner fella was here, the Taylors decided to get ready quick. It'll maybe be two hours or so before the kids arrive, but that fool saloon owner and his like may find out what's goin' on here. Can't take no chances. The cook is gettin' busy, at least the young 'uns won't starve.'

'Thanks, and pass along my thanks to the Taylors.' He gave the ranch hand a two-fingered salute, then looked at Angie Knowland, who was now past the gate looking back at him. They exchanged nods and then the pastor rode off.

Angie saw Brad and Madelynn Taylor coming out of their ranch house to greet her. She needed to focus on the job ahead. But inwardly she felt ashamed of herself for being so open with Nate Enders.

'I need to live in the real world and forget about dreams,' she whispered to herself.

CHAPTER TWELVE

Sahale had finished putting away the few utensils he had used to fix breakfast. An alert observer could spot the remains of a fire, but otherwise there was no indication that the chief of the Wichita had spent the night in this location. Sahale's caution was routine. He was a man with many enemies, both white and red-skinned.

'Hello the camp!'

The Chief's instincts caused him to tense up. Blackness still dominated the sky, with only faint wisps of gray moving in. But the figure on horseback wasn't trying to hide and the voice sounded familiar.

'Enter as a friend,' Sahale said.

Rance Dehner slowly rode in on his bay gelding. 'Good morning, Sahale, I've been riding my horse pretty hard, mind if I let him drink?' He nodded toward the stream a few yards away.

'You don't require my permission to use the stream,' the Indian laughed as he spoke.

Rance dismounted and began to walk the bay toward the water. 'I've just come from the Taylor ranch. They told me you stopped by there for a moment last night and that I could probably find you in this area.'

'Yes, I'm trying to locate a small herd of wild horses. I believe they are nearby. Once I find them, I will bring some young braves along to help me with the capture. Fort Williamson is expanding. The army will need more and more horses.'

Sahale paused for a moment and glanced around him as if fearful that someone was listening in. 'My father called the army enemies; I call them customers.'

Dehner left his horse at the stream and walked back toward the chief. 'I guess that's progress.'

'Perhaps, but that word "progress" always puts me on guard. When a white man speaks of progress it is rarely good news for Indians.'

There was nothing Dehner could say in response to that, and he didn't try. The detective simply smiled and nodded.

Sahale's good-natured mood returned. 'The day is coming when I will have competition when it comes to serving my customers. There are several tribes in this section of Texas. Soon, others will learn of the money to be made in selling horses. I want my braves to be prepared to deal with the army and the large ranchers. That is one reason I encourage my people to send their little ones to school. Angie Knowland is preparing them for what lies ahead.'

'That is why I have come, Sahale. The school is in danger.'

Dehner explained about the townspeople who were threatening to keep Indian children from the school. Sahale looked alarmed. 'Are you going to help deal with this mob?'

'More than help,' Dehner replied quickly. 'I've talked the marshal into allowing me to be the guy who talks to Howard Dixon and his buddies.'

'Why?'

'We're not dealing with criminals,' the detective explained. 'I want to believe Dixon and the rest are decent enough types who have gone crazy for the moment. If there's violence, it shouldn't be started by the marshal and his deputy. Shem Carson and Rip Gowdy will need to be part of the rebuilding when all this killing stops.'

'I hope there is no fighting,' Sahale concurred. 'But I must be there. I must stand with Nata and defend the school.'

'That's the way I thought you'd look at it,' Dehner said, as he looked at the stream and his horse. 'We've got some fast riding ahead of us.'

*

As Dehner and Sahale reigned up in front of the school the detective noted that he and the chief were joining up with ten other men. Dehner immediately recognized Shem Carson, Rip Gowdy, Reverend Nate, Jeremy Wilcox, Dade Knowland and, of course, Stacey Hooper. The other four men were merchants or ranchers; all four were fathers of children who attended the school.

'Welcome to the party, gents!' Carson exclaimed gleefully, before making quick introductions. 'We all need to be on a first name basis here.'

'When do our guests of honour arrive?' Dehner asked.

'Dade was keepin' a watch out for us from his store.' The marshal answered. 'He tells us that thirty minutes or so ago, a crowd of 'bout fifteen men were gatherin' in front of the Lucky Ace. They was passin' a bottle 'round to sorta bolster their courage. Reckon they'll be arrivin' soon.'

Carson went silent for a moment, obviously mulling matters over. 'Sahale, could you stay on your horse and keep guard on the left side of the building? I got Rip on his roan guardin' the right side. Our friends will be arrivin' on horseback, it might be a good idea for some of us to be likewise.'

Sahale nodded and took his place beside the school house.

The marshal shifted his gaze to Dehner and pointed his thumb to the right. 'Be a good idea for you to tie up your bay in those trees like the rest of us has done.'

Dehner complied, and as he walked back wasn't surprised that a sense of forced jocularity prevailed in front of the school. That was very often the case with men who were moments away from danger.

'Now fellas, I know your mommas would never allow you to have candy before a meal. They always said it would spoil your appetite.' Dade Knowland pulled a large sack out of his coat pocket. 'But I figger you're all growed up now. So I brought along some rock candy and gumdrops, even though most of you ain't had breakfast. Help yourselves!'

Loud laughter ensued as the men passed the bag around. Somebody tossed the sack to Rip Gowdy who caught it, put a gumdrop in his mouth, and then threw the bag back to the store owner.

'Thanks Dade, but it's a mighty shame ya didn't bring us some different treats. I know all 'bout your secret.'

Knowland looked confused. Rip chuckled before explaining, 'I was in the Red Eye one mornin' askin' that Lafe jasper 'bout a fight he'd been in the night before, when you came in. Lafe tole me you buy a jug from Sam ever' month. But only one a month, that's all ya need, guess candy does it for ya most days.'

The laughter became uneasy. Dade tried to smile, but his unhappiness at having his secret revealed was obvious. Both Shem Carson and Dehner felt frustrated with the deputy. He hadn't intended to create a ripple of discomfort, but he did, and this was not a time to distort the comradery in a group of men who might soon be fighting together.

They had to cool their emotions fast, as approaching horses sounded from not too far away. A waving dark line appeared against the reddening sky. As the line drew nearer threatening shouts could be heard.

The men in front of the school immediately became solemn and determined as they, too, arranged themselves in a line. A line that fronted the school: most of the men were holding rifles.

Rance Dehner was relying only on his holstered Colt .45. He took several steps forward and held up a hand. The oncoming riders stopped. They looked surprised.

'Sorry gents, but you all look a bit old to be attending school,' Dehner eyed the tacky collection of troublemakers. Most of them had been drinking. All of them looked jittery. They had not been expecting any resistance. The detective spoke in a calm, friendly manner, well aware that jittery men can do stupid things. 'So, why don't you fellas just go back to your jobs? You all have a lot more important things to do than scare off children. Let's forget this little incident happened. Everyone will be better off for it.'

'Jus' who are you, mister?' The question came from a large-boned man with an angular face and a head slightly too big for the rest of his body. He was sitting on a piebald beside Howard Dixon, who was perched on a buckskin.

'My name is Rance Dehner, and I have the pleasure of addressing?'

'Vince Bursey, I own the saddle shop. I've seen you around town, Dehner. You're friends with Hooper, the gambler.'

'Guilty as charged,' the detective replied.

'Just what's your stake in this game, Dehner?' Bursey leaned forward as he folded his hands on his saddle horn.

Rance smiled mockingly. 'I'm a strong believer in public education.'

'I think somebody needs to wipe that grin right off your face, Dehner, and I think I can handle the job just fine!' Bursey gave Howard Dixon a quick, hard glance as he dismounted. Bursey walked toward Dehner, caressing the gun on his hip.

He had intended the motion as a distraction. Bursey swung at Dehner with his left arm. The detective ducked and doubled up his adversary with a hard punch to his midriff. Spotting motion from the corner of his eye, Rance turned, drew his Colt and stabbed a flame into the shoulder of George Briggs, who was just lifting his gun from its holster.

Briggs plunged to the ground as his sorrel went up on its back legs. The horses near the sorrel neighed loudly and began to buck, their riders fighting for control.

Bursey's hand once again moved toward his holstered gun, only this time it wasn't a ploy. Dehner smashed his Colt against the man's head and Bursey went sprawling into the dust.

'Had enough?!' the detective shouted at the now broken line of riders in front of him. He was met with looks of confusion and remorse.

'Get out of here and don't bother this school again!' Dehner's second shout caused Howard Dixon to turn his steed and hastily ride off. The rest of the intruders, except for Vince Bursey and George Briggs, followed Dixon.

Dehner grabbed the gun from the holster of a moaning Vince Bursey. As he did, Shem Carson ran to where George Briggs lay bleeding. He picked up Briggs's gun and crouched over the wounded man as most of the volunteers formed a circle around the town's barber.

Stacey Hooper joined Dehner, who was helping Bursey to his feet. 'Rance, may I recommend you not press any charges against Mr Bursey?' The gambler looked to the sky. 'This is a matter that calls for the grace that flows through forgiveness. I can assure you that by extending Christian charity you will be helping this lost soul to realize the error of his wicked ways.'

Dehner quickly surveyed the scene. Shem Carson was giving instructions to the men around him. A messenger was being sent to the Taylor ranch with the news that the children could come to school, other men were being tasked with getting George Briggs to a doctor. Slightly outside the circle surrounding the barber stood Jeremy Wilcox. The reporter's head kept turning back to where Dehner was standing, as he also tried to take in everything the marshal was saying.

The detective refocused on the advice just given to him. 'How would it help Bursey if I didn't bring charges against him?'

Stacey lifted up an index finger. 'Mr Bursey's primary sin is stupidity.'

'You're right there!' Dehner folded his arms as he watched Vince Bursey, whose eyes were cast downward as he massaged the side of his head.

'Before your arrival in Conrad, I was a customer at Bursey's Saddle Shop,' Stacey explained. 'During this exercise in commerce I did business with Missus Bursey. She is a woman who tolerates no nonsense. I can assure you that when he returns home, Mr Bursey will be subjected to anguish far beyond what any jail cell could inflict.'

'OK.' Dehner once again smiled mockingly. 'Get back to your shop, Bursey, and keep your nose clean.'

Vince Bursey staggered away as the town's reporter ran up to Dehner. 'You letting Vince go?'

'Yes,' Dehner replied.

Wilcox stared at the retreating shop owner and apparently decided there was nothing of interest there. 'Marshal Carson said he wouldn't charge Briggs with anything, but he expected Briggs to start acting sensible...I have to get my equipment quick!'

'What do you mean?' Stacey asked.

'They're taking George to the doc's,' Wilcox flung his arms out. 'The sun is coming out and Doc Cunningham's office has a large window. I can get a picture of him patching up George...maybe the marshal and the deputy will be there too! The *Conrad Gazette* has a Pearsall, one of the most modern cameras made, and today I'm going to put it to good use!'

Stacey Hooper watched as the reporter ran for his horse. The gambler then turned to Rance, 'Ah, the charms of a small Western town.'

CHAPTER THIRTEEN

The figure walked slowly toward the Red Eye. Sun-up was a bad time for a break-in, but the Red Eye was a saloon, brothel and even a bit of a restaurant. The place never stood empty.

The figure ducked into the alley separating the Red Eye from Franklin's Hardware as the saloon door opened and a bald-headed man stepped cautiously out. The nervous gent had obviously spent the night in one of the upstairs rooms and was looking around, hoping no one would spot him leaving. Satisfied that his reputation was safe, he hurried off, not looking sideways to see the man in the alley.

The figure peered around the corner to watch Sam, who had apparently just unlocked the door, as she stepped on to the boardwalk outside her saloon and muttered something low and guttural. She seemed to be expressing hatred for the town and perhaps her life. The woman re-entered the saloon and slammed the door behind her.

The figure remained in the alley for a few minutes as a man in overalls rode by, heading for the livery. He then approached the door of the saloon and opened it slightly. Sam had left it unlocked. A glance inside revealed no one. The intruder eased inside, navigating the bat wings behind the main door carefully. He knew from experience that the bat wings squeaked when pushed hard.

The downstairs was empty. It wouldn't be that way long. The cook would be arriving soon.

From upstairs a woman began screaming, and a moment later there was the sound of a door hitting the wall as it was flung open. Sam's voice scorched the air with curses, and loud footsteps could be heard clomping down the hall as she ended her obscenities with, 'Lafe, wake the hell up!'

The intruder smiled inwardly. Luck was with him. He had originally planned to work his mischief on the ground floor, but maybe he could hit closer to home.

He moved slowly up the stairway on the far right side of the Red Eye as voices came from the left side of the upstairs hall. A young female voice screeched: 'This buzzard promised to pay me in the morning, but when I asked for the money he hit me.'

'You stupid little... always demand the money first... Lafe, get in here!' Sam's voice was still loud, but now muffled – she was inside a room.

The intruder reached the top of the stairway and saw that the last room down the hall was open, and so was the room nearest him, which had to be the room Sam had emerged from while moving in a cloud of curses.

From the far room came a whiny plea. 'I jus' didn't want to spend the night alone. I'm sorry, Sam.'

'You're gonna be plenty sorry,' came the saloon owner's reply. 'Ya see, Lafe don't like havin' ta get up early. Puts him in a right bad mood. Show this lousy mouse whatcha do when you're in a bad mood, Lafe.'

Once again, screams came from the room, but this time from a man. First a desperate cry for mercy, and then anguished screams of pain, accompanied by Sam's laughter. The noise covered the intruder's footsteps as he moved into Sam's room, carried out his plan, then quickly moved back down the stairs and out the door.

*

Sam looked at the pathetic creature who was writhing in pain on the floor. 'Lafe, throw out the garbage.'

Lafe picked up the semi-conscious man and dragged him out of the room. Sam looked at Sissy, or rather, the fifteen-year-old girl who had taken on that name. Sissy had pulled a thin blanket off the bed and wrapped it around her. Despite the cover, Sissy's entire body was shaking. Her left eye was already swelling and turning purple from the hit it had just absorbed.

'Ya demand the money first…remember that!' Sam pointed a threatening finger as she spoke.

'Yes, ma'am' Sissy replied.

'Ya pull somethin' stupid like that again and I'll let Lafe have a little fun with ya. I think Lafe enjoys beatin' up girls even more than boys.'

Panic covered Sissy's face. 'I won't ma'am, please, I promise.'

Sam gave the young woman an angry stare and then stomped off. But she returned to her room in a good mood, or as close to a good mood as Sam could get. She had triumphed over both a man and a girl, leaving both of them terrified of her.

Sam's good mood vanished the moment she stepped into her room. On one wall, in big letters, was scrawled the word 'Coyote'.

CHAPTER FOURTEEN

Dade Knowland sat on a stool behind the counter of his store trying to work on account books. His real attention was focused on Angie, who was hurriedly working behind him, taking cans of peaches from a crate and arranging them on a shelf. Dade knew his daughter often took on such tasks when she was distraught.

'Forget about them cans,' Dade tried to sound casual. 'I can see to it later.'

'It's not a problem, Father.'

'Don't you need to look over your lesson plans for tomorrow?' Dade found it harder to keep the concern from his voice.

Angie grimaced as she straightened the cans, making sure the labels faced forward. 'I'm going to use the same lessons I was supposed to teach today.'

'I don't unnerstand.'

'The kids were so excited when we moved them from the Taylor ranch to the school that I spent most of the day trying to calm them down.' Angie grabbed two more cans from the crate. 'And it was all my fault.'

71

'Bull! It weren't your fault!'

'The children wanted to know why everything was so different, and I wouldn't tell them.' The teacher paused and then continued. 'Hiding the truth never works.'

'Angie, don't you think…'

There was a loud knock on the front door. The moon was bright and most of the lanterns outside of the town's stores were still burning. From the glass pane in the top half of the door, Dade spotted a vaguely familiar face. He pointed at the closed sign in the store's main window.

The man at the door shook his head and knocked again. Dade got up from his stool, walked quickly around the counter and opened the door just far enough to speak. 'Sorry, we're closed…'

'I ain't here 'bout nothin' like that, I gotta message from the Taylors!'

Dade now recognized the man standing in front of him. His name was Jack, and he was a ranch hand for the Taylors. He had been at the store a couple of times helping Brad Taylor to pick up supplies.

Angie hurried to her father's side, as surprised as he was by Jack's statement. The store owner shrugged his shoulders slightly before replying, 'Well…ah…what's the message?'

'They want ya both out ta the ranch tonight – quick!'

Both father and daughter now looked confused. Angie asked the next question: 'Is this something about their daughter, Maddie? She seemed fine in school today.'

'Don't know. All I can say is they tole me to ask you folks to get right out there. Can I tell 'em you're comin'?'

'Yes, of course,' Dade glanced quickly at his daughter who nodded her head. 'We'll get goin' at once.'

Jack touched an index finger to his hat and left. Dade closed the door and shook his head. 'I can't unnerstan why Brad and Madelynn are so fired up 'bout seein' us.'

'I guess we'll have to ride out there and find out.'

Dade smiled at the practicality of his daughter's statement. 'Guess so.' But his smile quickly vanished and didn't return as they locked up the store and headed for the small stable out back.

Both Knowlands were anxious about the strange request they had received, but their anxiety was offset by the pleasant evening, which made their ride enjoyable. About fifteen minutes from the Taylor ranch, Angie slowed the pace of her black and pointed forward.

'Father, beside that large boulder there's a horse with a saddle on it...and something is lying beside it.'

Dade also slowed his horse and leaned forward. His eyes were not as good as those of his daughter. 'Yeh, looks like a man, his horse must have throwed him and then he hit the boulder. He's probably unconscious.'

Father and daughter rode a bit closer to the scene, dismounted, ground tethered their horses, and walked briskly toward the fallen rider. Dade crouched over the body and gave a surprised laugh. 'This ain't no man, it's a lotta straw stuffed in a man's clothes.'

Angie looked at the saddled grey behind them. 'Then who does the horse belong to?'

A massive figure stepped out from behind the boulder holding a rifle. 'The grey is mine, and you two are joinin' me for a little ride.'

CHAPTER FIFTEEN

Dade Knowland rode his horse slowly down a small hill toward a dilapidated line shack that was sandwiched between two other small hills. His daughter rode beside him. Riding behind him was Lafe, who cradled a rifle with his right arm. Lafe was not wearing a mask, which left Dade terrified for his daughter and himself. The brute didn't care if they could identify him, which could only mean one thing...

'Stop here, git off your horses!'

Both Knowlands obeyed the order. They were in front of the shack. As they ground tethered their horses, Dade spotted the remains of whiskey bottles scattered all about. The glass had collected layers of dirt. Whatever merriment had taken place here was long ago in the past.

They stepped into the smoke-filled cabin, which contained no windows. Sam puffed on a cigarette as she sat on the shack's only chair in front of the only table. There was no other furniture. A lantern perched on the dust-covered table; beside the light was a small satchel.

Sam's face appeared brooding, and for several minutes she didn't speak. The woman looked at the tobacco smoke, which twirled around her like a hostile army.

The quiet unnerved even Lafe, who said, 'I brung 'em, like ya said.'

The owner of the Red Eye looked at her hired muscle with contempt. The derision stayed in her eyes as they shifted to Dade Knowland. 'Ya couldn't leave it alone, could ya?'

'I don't know what you mean,' the store owner replied.

Sam couldn't comprehend the sincerity in Dade's words. 'We had a nice little arrangement. You'd pay me once a month, and I'd keep quiet 'bout your little buttercup. But no, you tried to scare me off. Well, you're 'bout to learn I don't scare!'

'I never tried to scare you, Sam!' Dade tried to remain calm. He sensed he was fighting for his life and the life of his daughter. 'I always pay on time. I even buy a jug from you. I figgered the folks who worked at the Red Eye would wonder why I came in ever month. I never missed a payment, never will.'

Hatred penetrated Sam's eyes, piercing through the smoke. 'Ya thought I was some scared little rabbit, like Mona Clement. Ya wrote "Coyote" on the wall of my room this mornin'. Guess ya figgered I'm superstitious...frightened of monsters under my bed... I'd run outta town and never come back. Well, mister respectable store-keep, you and your buttercup are 'bout to find out different.'

'I don't know what you're talkin' 'bout.' Dade looked at his daughter, whose frightened face indicated she was also ignorant as to what had caused Sam's venomous ranting.

Sam waved a hand in Dade's direction, causing red embers to flare into the semi-darkness then vanish. 'If ya didn't do it, who in hell did?'

'I don't know!' Dade shouted.

The overweight woman looked confused as she slowly stood up. 'Maybe ya did, maybe ya didn't. I ain't takin' chances, I'm killin' both of ya.'

The store owner's voice became a plea. 'There's no need to hurt Angie, please—'

Sam's voice became a loud roar. 'I knew I'd hafta kill the whore when I decided ta kill you. She'd know who did the killin'.'

Dade silently rebuked himself for trying to plead for mercy from a woman who didn't have any. Something different was needed, 'Kill us, Sam, and the money stops!'

The smile that cut Sam's face didn't contain a trace of humor. 'I'll still make money off of ya, Dade. Ya never shoulda pulled that banker outta his office and beat him up in broad daylight. He tole me if I ever found ya to have ya done away with, and he'd reward me with five hundred dollars...but I'd hafta keep quiet 'bout it. After all, he's a respectable banker.'

As the false smile vanished from the older woman's face, Angie realized that every time the saloon owner used the word 'respectable' it crawled out of her mouth like a vicious obscenity. Angie Knowland briefly closed her eyes and whispered to herself, 'You fool!'

'Yep, a respectable banker don't go 'round hirin' killers, the word could git out.' Sam said. 'He trusts me 'cause I never tried to backmail him. He tole me if I found ya and had ya killed it would mean a nice little pay-off.'

Sam dropped the stub that was left of her smoke and then reached into her pocket and pulled out a tobacco pouch. She cursed upon seeing that the pouch was empty and stuffed it back in her pocket.

'I got me some...'

Sam cut off Lafe's offer. 'Keep that Sharps and Hanker pointed where it is. Ya can give me the makins in a few minutes.'

The owner of the Red Eye opened the satchel on the desk and shook it. A large knife fell out. 'All this is happenin' at a right convenient time. Lafe here is gonna cut the two of ya up somethin' fierce. Then, we'll dump what's left of your bodies behind your store. Ever one will blame that Coyote.'

'Do you know what's behind all this Coyote talk?' Dade asked.

'Naaa, but that don't make no never mind. After your bodies are found, that Wilcox jasper will want ta take some pictures. I'll send one of them pictures to my banker friend.'

The smile returned to Sam's face. 'Ya know, I'm gonna sorta enjoy watching Lafe at work. Yep, Lafe is…'

A cracking sound caused Sam's eyes to dart fearfully to the front of the shack where Rance Dehner's body crashed through the thin door and hit the floor. 'Drop the rifle, Lafe!'

Lafe had just started to swing the Sharps and Hanker toward Dehner when a bullet from the detective's gun speared into the brute's leg. Lafe crumpled in pain and his body did a half turn as he pressed down on the trigger of his rifle. The shot exploded into Sam's head.

Lafe staggered toward her body lying on the floor. He pushed aside the small table and stood over Sam's remains. He made a loud bellow, which could have been anger, despair or some emotion only he could understand. The large man then turned toward Dehner, who was now standing, gun in hand.

'Drop the rifle, Lafe, last warning,' Dehner snapped.

Lafe began to lift the Sharps and Hanker in Dehner's direction, but was stopped by another bullet, this one in the chest. Lafe remained on his feet with a look of shock and fury on his now ashen face.

Stacey Hooper stepped into the shack, pistol in hand, and quickly fired four bullets into Lafe. The large brute went down after absorbing Stacey's fourth shot. The gambler then hastily walked over to the fallen giant and speared one more bullet into him.

'Insurance,' the gambler declared.

There was something in the offhand buoyancy of Hooper's comment that angered Dehner. 'Did you have to…'

'Yes,' came Stacey's firm reply. 'These two were evil people who should be buried and forgotten. They would have come to a bad end sooner or later. Better sooner.'

Rance was in no mood to argue with his friend. He looked at Dade and Angie, who were just getting up. Dade had pushed his daughter to the floor and then crouched over her as a shield against bullets.

'I'm sorry,' Dehner said. 'This is all my fault.'

'Your fault?!' Despite the circumstances, Angie managed a laugh. 'Mr Dehner, you just saved our lives. This morning some ruffian wrote "Coyote" on the wall of Sam's room, and she thought it was Father. She was about to kill us.'

'That's what I was talking about,' Rance explained. 'I'm the ruffian, the one who snuck into the Red Eye and wrote "Coyote" on Sam's wall.'

CHAPTER SIXTEEN

'And I shall dwell in the house of the Lord for ever.'

'Amen,' Angie's voice was soft and reverent. 'Thank you for reciting the twenty-third psalm, Rance. Stacey is right. Sam and Lafe were evil people. But it just seemed wrong to bury them without some words being spoken.'

Angie, her father, Rance and Stacey stood around two freshly dug graves beside the deserted line shack. Hooper was holding the lantern which had been on the table in the shack. The sense of relief that followed the killings of Sam and Lafe and the task of burying them had brought on a new sense of closeness between the four people.

Dade waved his hands nervously in front of him. 'Rance, I don't mean to come across as not being grateful but...'

Dehner finished the question for him. 'Why did I write "Coyote" on the wall of Sam's room?'

'Well...yes,' Dade answered.

'Because I was desperate and didn't know what else to do.' Dehner gave a sigh of self-loathing.

'Don't be so hard on yourself, good friend,' Stacey chirped. 'No sense in dwelling on life's little shortcomings.'

Angie glanced at the graves, then looked up at the living. 'I don't understand.'

79

Rance spoke directly to the young woman. 'This morning, while we were guarding the school, Rip Gowdy kidded your father about buying a jug every month from the Red Eye. Your father's face reflected a strong reaction to something that was an innocent joke.'

Angie again closed her eyes, this time as if absorbing a blow. 'And you became suspicious.'

'Not exactly,' Dehner confessed. 'But this whole situation with Akando has me baffled.'

'Indeed!' Stacey proclaimed in his usual cheerful manner. The lantern in his hand seemed to put him in a spotlight. 'When my friend feels that he has hit a dead end in a case, he often pulls a prank of some kind in order to prod some of the participants in the matter into action. His little stunt this morning in the Red Eye certainly succeeded in that regard!'

The detective shifted his eyes between the two Knowlands, 'I didn't realize I was putting your lives in so much danger. I'm sorry.'

Both father and daughter mumbled kind words, which were interrupted by Stacey. 'What a shame it would be if Rance's efforts resulted in no new information being revealed. Dade, surely you want...'

'Nothin' I say will help end this situation with Akando!' Dade Knowland hoped that his statement would end the discussion.

Angie destroyed her father's hopes. 'I want to tell them.'

Desperation shot from Dade's eyes, 'Angie, please...'

'I'm tired of pretending I'm something I'm not,' the young woman replied.

There was an uneasy silence, which Dade broke. 'Angie and I use ta live in another town not too far aways from here, but not too close. I ran a store, Angie helped out.

There was a drought, a bad one, and many of the ranchers couldn't pay up on the credit I gave them. I couldn't make my payments to the bank.'

Dehner looked a bit surprised. 'Most bankers in the West carry people through hard times like droughts. That's how banking works in this part of the country.'

'Many bankers do,' Dade agreed, 'But not Carl Udall. That snake saw a chance to grab up a store, which would be makin' a profit again in six months or thereabouts, and he went after me. Then, suddenly he let up. At first, I didn't know why.'

There was another silence, this time Angie spoke up. 'Sam lived in that town. She ran a brothel. Carl Udall was one of her steady customers. Apparently, Mr Udall told Sam that he found me attractive. One afternoon, while Father was working in the back room, Sam came into the store and offered me a deal. If I…visited…Mr Udall once a week he would stop threatening Father.'

'She was only sixteen at the time!' Dade shouted angrily.

'I knew what I was doing.' Angie whispered.

'How long did this go on?' Dehner asked.

'Three weeks,' the store keeper said. 'One afternoon, Angie came back from seein' a friend, or that bein' what she tole me. One side of her face was bruised. Udall liked to get rough. It took a while, but I got the truth outta my daughter. Damn! I ran to the bank, dragged Udall out on to the street and beat the hell outta him.'

'What happened next?' Stacey sounded genuinely curious.

'We had ta leave town before sun-up the next mornin',' Dade answered. 'Udall was an important gent, the law would be comin' after me.'

Angie sighed deeply, 'Carl Udall was able to take over the store after all.'

'Did you come to Conrad right away?' Dehner asked.

Dade shook his head. 'No, we travelled 'round doin' odd jobs, but when we hit Conrad it looked like our luck had changed. The bank had jus' took over the general store, which was failin'. The banker here is a good fella, he talked with me some and made me the manager of the store. I made it profitable, and was able to buy it from the bank. Meanwhiles, Angie became the schoolmarm. Things seemed to be goin' good.'

'Then Sam arrived,' Dehner said.

'Yeh,' came the store owner's quick reply.

Rance tugged at his ear. 'The way I figure it, Udall staked Sam to a certain amount of money. She was to locate you and arrange for your murder. But when Sam found you in Conrad, she followed a different plan. She bought the Red Eye, set up business, and began a blackmail scheme. In the long run, blackmail would bring in more money than the five hundred Udall promised her. Then I started playing games, and everything went crazy.'

'I'm glad you did what you did, Rance.' Angie looked up at the dark sky and then seemed to look at nothing. 'I have already told Reverend Nate that this will be my final year teaching school. I will repeat my decision to him tomorrow. I will also stop playing the piano on Sunday. No one with my background should be sitting on the platform of the church in front of everybody.'

Dehner gave the young woman a wistful smile. 'I suggest you tell the Reverend why you are doing so much resigning.'

Angie's face contorted and tears began to dampen her cheeks. 'I can't do that!'

'Yes, you can,' Rance Dehner said.

CHAPTER SEVENTEEN

'Today is Wednesday,' Dehner spoke in a morose voice.

'You've always been great with details, my friend,' Stacey Hooper grinned over a cup of coffee. 'That's what makes you such a fine detective.'

After returning from the line shack, Rance, Stacey and both of the Knowlands woke up Shem Carson who was sleeping on a cot in his office, and told him what had happened. Rip Gowdy listened in. Dehner confessed to scrawling 'Coyote' on the wall of Sam's room. Dade admitted that the saloon owner had been blackmailing him over 'Something that took place long ago', but his strident voice indicated he would say no more about the blackmail. Shem Carson accepted that for the time being.

The marshal was now seated at a table in Ma Trent's restaurant, eating breakfast along with Rance and Stacey, both of whom had grabbed about three hours of sleep. Dehner stirred his black cup of coffee. 'Today is Wednesday,' he repeated. 'Akando's ultimatum runs out in five days. The situation with Sam wasn't connected to Akando at all.'

'But you have uncovered truths that needed to be brought into the sunlight, and have thus served the high cause of justice!' Stacey's eyes shot upwards as if gazing at the high cause. 'Don't you agree, Marshal?'

'Suppose so,' Carson muttered. 'If it makes you feel any better, Rance, you was right 'bout Jack, the Taylors' ranch hand.'

'He'd been fired by Brad Taylor?' Dehner asked.

'Yep.' The marshal chewed on his steak before continuing. 'Jack was hangin' 'round the Red Eye doin' a lotta nothin'. Sam gave him five bucks to lie to the Knowlands. I gave him an hour to leave town for good. He kicked up some dust, but soon saw the wisdom of goin' along.'

From behind the restaurant's counter, Ma Trent, a large-boned, red-headed woman, stared accusingly at her only three customers. Why, it was getting on to ten am, and decent folks should be at their jobs.

Dehner noted the disapproval, but decided to ignore it. 'I do have another truth to bring into the sunlight.'

Stacey's eyebrows went up. He assumed the new truth would provide a source of enjoyment. 'Please do share it with us.'

Dehner complied. 'On my first day in town, I sent a telegram to the Lowrie Detective Agency in Dallas, asking my boss to do some checking on Jeremy Wilcox. I just received a reply.'

'Aha!' Hooper declared mockingly. 'You are not on an official case, and yet Bertram Lowrie did background work for you. Like me, Mr Lowrie is obviously a man who believes in truth for truth's sake. What new facts have emerged?'

Rance lowered his voice. 'Wilcox is a liar – sort of.'

Shem stared into his coffee cup, and then stared at Dehner. 'You're gonna haf' ta spell it out a bit more for this old lawdog.'

Rance kept his voice low. 'Jeremy told us his father bought the *Dallas Chronicle* in order to fire his son and force him into the business world. Exactly the opposite happened: Jeremy's dad bought the *Chronicle* and Jeremy was hired almost the next day.'

Carson sipped his coffee before asking, 'So, Wilcox wasn't fired from the newspaper?'

'Not by his father,' Dehner answered.

The marshal looked confused, 'Well, then…'

Dehner continued. 'Jeremy punched an editor who criticized his work and was fired immediately. There was nothing his father could do.'

Silence followed, but as was usually the case with Stacey Hooper around, the silence was brief. 'As I see it, Mr Jeremy Wilcox is following a very familiar pattern.'

Rance smiled in a resigned manner. 'And exactly what is this pattern?'

'Jeremy Wilcox feels guilty for being born into wealth,' Stacey said. 'So he tries to portray himself as the poor little rich boy. His mother died when he was an infant, and Jeremy was at the cruel whims of a rich robber baron. He is more to be pitied then censured.'

Marshal Carson nodded his head. 'Makes sense. Now Wilcox is tryin' to prove he can still be a good newspaper man even without his pappy's help.'

Another silence followed, and this time Dehner ended it. 'What can you tell me about Charlie Bell, Shem?'

The lawman shrugged his shoulders. 'I tend to look the other way with moonshiners. Charlie ain't in town that much. Mona Clement tole me her husband had taken business away from Charlie: the Red Eye and a few ranches. I can't believe Bell would kill over that. But, then, I wouldn't have thought folks in this town would think killin's could be done by some spook named Coyote.'

'Maybe Stacey and I should call on Charlie Bell.'

'Obliged,' Shem Carson answered, and then gave directions to Bell's still as the threesome departed from Ma Trent's. 'I ain't been there for a few years…'

'Marshal!' The shout came from Jeremy Wilcox. The reporter dismounted from his buckskin, leaving the horse standing in the middle of the street. The lathered animal used the opportunity to blow and paw the dust. Wilcox quickly ran to join the threesome standing outside the restaurant.

'I just rode past the bank,' Wilcox declared breathlessly, 'Howard Dixon is inside there!'

The marshal grimaced before speaking, though Rance thought he detected a trace of interest in the lawman's voice. 'The way you talk, sounds like Howard is robbin' the place.'

The lack of seriousness in the marshal's response angered Jeremy, but he kept it in check. 'The way I see it, with Sam dead, Howard Dixon is negotiating to take ownership of the Red Eye. He'll own the two biggest saloons in town!'

Carson shrugged his shoulders, 'Nothin' illegal 'bout that. I tole Freemont, the banker, what had happened; he probably tole Howard.'

The reporter appeared irked. He had just come up with a major scoop and no one seemed to care.

Dehner cared, but not about Howard Dixon. 'How did you know Sam was dead, Jeremy?'

''Fraid that was my doin',' Carson said. 'While I was convincin' Jack to leave town, I tole him how Sam and Lafe got themselves killed.' The lawman pointed at Wilcox. 'This gent was listenin' in.'

'You were talking with that Jack character on the boardwalk, Marshal.' Wilcox replied indignantly. 'I had every right to listen in.'

The marshal gave a curt nod. 'I ain't sayin' otherwise.'

Wilcox continued to prod the lawman. 'I have a friend I used to work with in Dallas. He's with the *New York Globe* now. We've exchanged telegrams. The *Globe* is very interested in the Coyote story. They want me to serve as their correspondent!'

'Excellent, Jeremy!' Stacey declared. 'Now the denizens of this nation's largest city will soon be following the events right here in Conrad, Texas. A magnificent city, New York, as I can attest from my brief but illustrious career in the theater.'

Now, Dehner's eyebrows shot up. 'You used to be an actor?!'

'Indeed,' Stacey answered. 'There are still people who talk about my performance in *Hamlet*.'

Rance continued to be shocked. 'You played the Danish prince?!'

'No, I played Guildenstern and was terribly underpaid. I made up for my scandalously low stipend in card games with the cast and crew. That was when I decided on a new career.' Hooper steadied his gaze on the lawman. 'But Marshal, you should be pleased a town as important as New York is taking an interest in Conrad, Texas.'

'Them folks in New York may join the chorus and start hoorawin' me 'bout catchin' some ghost,' Carson looked accusingly at the newspaper owner. 'I hope you'll use more sense in the future articles you write about Coyote.'

'I hope you are not trying to influence the work of a free press, Marshall,' Jeremy declared.

Shem Carson shook his head and walked away.

CHAPTER EIGHTEEN

'According to Shem Carson, we should be arriving at Charlie Bell's business enterprise any moment now. We've been riding for over an hour.' When Stacey received no response to his statement he looked at his companion. 'You seem to be very interested in the ground, Rance. Spot any silver nuggets?'

'No. But I do spot some unshod horse prints. A lot of Indians have been by here.'

'That's hardly a surprise, my good friend. Indians enjoy the devil's brew as much as anyone else.'

Dehner appeared unconvinced by Stacey's logic. He pointed to his right. 'Let's take a walk up that hill and see what we can see.'

Both men tied their horses to trees at the bottom of the hill, and made their way upwards on foot with field glasses hung around their necks. At the top, both men lay down and employed the glasses. They could see that the hill horseshoed around two large buildings and a barn. All of the structures were clapboard, and had been recently constructed.

'The layout is quite curious,' said Stacey, surprise obvious in his voice. 'Usually a moonshiner is thought of as operating out of a half-collapsed shed, surrounded by a family that bathes every Christmas. The still must be in one of those buildings, but what's in the other one?'

'I don't know,' Rance confessed. 'But there's a crew at work there. We need to get an exact count. And take a look at those wagons beside the barn: nothing cheap about Charlie Bell's business – those wagons cost plenty.'

Stacey gave a lopsided smile. 'I guess a moonshiner is entitled to climb the ladder of success.'

'Good thing we had a big breakfast,' Dehner said.

Stacey Hooper moaned. 'I guess you mean we are going to be here observing Charlie Bell Enterprises for the rest of the day and, no doubt, well into the night.'

'Yes,' Dehner answered. 'But first let's go down and hide our horses as best we can. I have a feeling we're not among friends.'

*

'Miss Knowland, I must express my appreciation for the wonderful work you do on the piano.'

The voice startled Angie. She had been lost in private thoughts as she sat at the piano closing the hymnals she had just used for the Wednesday night prayer meeting. 'Ah…thank you Mr Wilcox, you're very kind.'

'The West very much needs people with your wonderful talents.'

Angie felt she should respond with a remark about journalists being a valuable asset to the West, but she feared giving Jeremy Wilcox encouragement. She settled for a smile indicating gratitude.

That was enough encouragement for Jeremy. 'I do wish you'd allow me to do a piece about your work at the school.

You know, the big Eastern newspapers are already picking up my articles about Coyote, and I'm sure…'

'I'm sorry, Mr Wilcox, but we've already talked about this…'

Jeremy had anticipated the answer and was ready with a response. 'Perhaps I could change your mind over a nice…'

The young woman raised her voice to cut off the invitation: 'Mr Wilcox, please excuse me, but I am a bit tired at the moment.'

'Yes, of course.' A flash of disappointment ran across Jeremy's face, but it was only a flash. He smiled politely before stepping off the platform.

As she watched him leave the church, Angie felt sorry for the newspaperman. Perhaps she should show more interest in him. He seemed an ambitious, likeable man, if a bit obnoxious at times. Why had she rebuffed his attempts to get close to her?

Angie knew the answer to that question, and whispered to herself, 'I've got to end my friendship with Nate, and end it now.'

With Jeremy gone, there were two men left in the church: Nate and Shem Carson. From what she could hear, they were discussing the fact that Rance Dehner and Stacey Hooper had not attended the meeting. She could hear Nate saying, 'If they're not back by morning, I'll ride with you out to Charlie Bell's place.'

Angie smiled inwardly. Reverend Nate and Marshal Carson were obviously concerned with anything Rance and Stacey had discovered in regard to the Coyote matter, rather than being worried about spiritual shortcomings that may have kept them from the prayer meeting.

She sighed, and turned her mind to more immediate matters as Shem Carson left the church. She stood up and began to place the two hymnals she had used for the service back into the piano bench.

Reverend Nate smiled as he walked toward her. 'I'll ride with you to the store, Angie.'

She closed the bench too quickly, sending a loud bang into the air. 'That won't be necessary, Reverend Nate, but thank you.'

'It'll be no trouble at all…please.'

She stepped off the platform, walked by the pastor and then turned and faced him. 'Reverend Nate, this Sunday will be the last time I play the piano in this church. I hope I have given you adequate time to find a replacement.'

'What?!' Nate was stunned and responded in a way he immediately regretted. 'This isn't Dallas or Denver. I can't find another pianist in a week or so!'

'I'm sorry,' Angie's face contorted as she began to walk away.

With three long strides, Nate slipped ahead and stood between Angie and the door. 'Please Angie, we need to talk.'

'I'll do what I can to help you find a replacement…'

'Hush!' Nate cried. 'Look, I apologize for all that replacement nonsense I just spouted. There are a lot more important matters involved here.'

Angie's eyes watered. 'No! There are not!'

'You're lying,' Nate shot back. 'You're not a stupid woman. You must have sensed that I'm falling in love with you. Last Sunday you stood up in this church and talked about the importance of truth. Well, now is the time for truth, Angie!'

CHAPTER NINETEEN

'The lights are out in both buildings,' Dehner said. 'I think our moonshiners are settled down for the night.'

'I do envy them,' Hooper replied.

'Time to test my theory,' Dehner raised his body into a crouch. 'I'll go down first; you know what to do.'

'I don't mean to discourage your fine efforts, good friend, but shouldn't we have a back-up plan, in case your theory is incorrect?'

'The only possible back-up plan is to shoot our way out.'

'My worst fears confirmed,' Hooper sighed.

Still crouching, Dehner made his way cautiously down the hill, which consisted primarily of gravel and a few struggling plants that couldn't make it above ankle level. When he reached flat ground the detective moved around to the back of the two buildings. From one he could sniff an unpleasant sweetness. He knew what was there and moved to the next building.

Dehner slowed as he approached a wide, open window. Pausing beside the window, he was certain he knew why the people inside were cavalier about leaving the glassless window open. They took turns doing a watch. Rance began to have second thoughts. Stacey's idea about a back-up plan really wasn't bad at all.

But an odour different from that produced by moonshine wafted from inside, giving the detective confidence in his theory. *Now, to begin the charade,* Dehner thought, as he climbed through the window without too much caution. He needed to create the illusion of an intruder breaking into a building he thought was deserted.

Despite the tension, Rance felt an inner joy as he spotted the outline of a printing press in the darkness. He lit a match and made his way to two large crates. Both contained empty bottles. Dehner got down on one knee and pulled a bottle from one of the crates. The label on the glass container almost looked like the real thing.

Something cold and hard pressed against the detective's neck. 'Put up your hands or I kill you.'

The man holding the rifle was bent over his target. Dehner spoke with a casual friendliness as he tossed away the match. 'Sure, whatever you say.'

Dehner's arms bolted up, hitting his adversary on the head with the bottle. The man yelled in a language Dehner couldn't understand as he stumbled backwards.

'Freeze, stranger!'

Dehner froze. He was still on one knee.

'Now keep those hands in the air, drop the bottle, get up slowly and turn around.' The voice giving the orders chuckled in a sinister manner. 'Right now you got three guns pointin' at you, and Wolf here is feelin' embarrassed over lettin' you trick him. Try another trick and we'll let Wolf take off your head with his Winchester. My, but Wolf does love that rifle.'

Dehner did what he was told and grinned in a friendly manner as he assessed his captors as best he could using the available moonlight. The man who had been giving the orders was tall and thin with pale skin covering a bony face that, even in the darkness, made him look sickly. The other two armed men were young Indians, probably a year or so short of twenty. Dehner assumed that 'Wolf' was short for an Indian name.

The front door of the building flew open and three other young Indians ran in. One of them spoke as he looked about, 'We hear noise.'

'You heard noise all right, Eagle, but we got things under control.'

Eagle appeared angered by having his name shortened, but said nothing. The one man in the room who was not an Indian was in charge.

The new arrivals were armed and had obviously run in from the other building. There were now five Indians and the boss man in the same building. That should be everyone involved in the operation. Dehner hoped he had gotten the count right.

'Who are you?' the sickly looking man asked.

'My name is Dehner. I'm a detective. I assume I am addressing Mr Charlie Bell?'

One of the Indians lit two lanterns which hung from a side wall. The light revealed a confused look on the boss man's face. 'Yeh, I'm Charlie Bell. Who are you workin' for, Dehner?'

A loud shout came from outside the window. 'I can answer that question, but first, I want everyone to drop their armaments. Then we can proceed in the manner of businessmen. There is money to be made here and we must not waste another minute on side issues.'

Bell looked at Stacey Hooper who stood outside the window with a Sharps and Hanker pointed inside. Stacey nodded at him in a polite, deferential manner. Bell dropped his pistol and gestured at the Indians to do the same with their Winchesters.

Stacey quickly made it through the window, rifle in hand. But he pointed the Sharps and Hanker at the floor as he approached Charlie, right hand extended. 'My name is Stacey Hooper, Mr Bell, I am the new owner of the Red Eye Saloon.'

Bell smiled as he shook hands with the gambler. 'I heard this mornin' that Sam and Lafe went to meet their maker. You don't waste no time, Mr Hooper.'

'Please, call me Stacey, and may I call you Charlie?'

'Yeh, sure,' Charlie replied. 'Always like to do business with a gent who is high hat.'

'I prefer to think of myself as thorough: a man who never overlooks anything. That's how I was able to outmaneuver Howard Dixon and grab ownership of the Red Eye.'

Bell laughed in a contemptuous manner. 'Dixon is like Sam in a lotta ways. He's big talk, can't keep quiet about nothin'. That's why I never did much business with him.'

Stacey handed his rifle to Rance, who now stood less than three feet away. The movement was casual, handing a no longer needed weapon over to the hired help. Stacey's joy in the moment was reflected in his voice. 'You provided Howard with a few jugs, from what I understand.'

'Small change stuff,' Charlie was getting in line with Stacey's approach. 'My moonshine wasn't as good as some others. I started out with the usual tanglefoot, but then smartened up and began makin' stuff closer to the legal booze. Less kick…I kept supplying Howard 'cause I didn't want to do anything to attract attention from Shem Carson. But I wanted to get outta sellin' jugs. Tried to find out from Sam who else was sellin' tanglefoot so I could give Howard's business to them, but for once, Sam kept her mouth shut.'

'Would you care for a cigar?' Stacey offered as he reached into his coat pocket.

'Sure,' Charlie answered, gesturing toward a table the perfect size for playing cards. 'Why don't we take a load off?'

As the two businessmen sat down and lit up, Rance observed the five Indians, who were still too young to mask their emotions. The looks on their faces reflected anger, and something else the detective couldn't peg, confusion perhaps. In any event, they were not happy.

Bell inhaled on the cigar Stacey had given him and looked at it appreciatively. 'You know, Stacey, it's right surprisin' how impressed some jaspers can be by a fancy label on a proper bottle. I figger'd that out a few years ago, and it's gonna make me rich.'

'How many places are you selling your booze to, Charlie?' Stacey's voice remained jolly but he was being cautious. He was approaching difficult questions that could blow the whole charade to bits.

'Mostly small towns right now, places like Trail's End. I gotta be careful like, can't take over too many saloons all

at once. The regular distributors might start to smell a rat.'
Bell gave his companion a questioning stare. 'Say, Stacey,
how'd you figger me out?'

Hooper laughed as if greatly amused by the question.
'Unlike most of your customers, I am a connoisseur of
the devil's brew. Being a gambler, I am also a travelling
man. I believe it was in Trail's End where I noticed something not quite right about the whiskey. I studied the
label, which only heightened my suspicions. I turned
the matter over to a detective, Rance Dehner, whom you
have already met. Dehner's investigation brought us to
Conrad.'

Some of the cordiality was beginning to slip from Charlie
Bell's eyes. 'You've put yourself through a lotta trouble.'

'And for a very good reason,' Stacey chirped back.
'I have often dreamed of owning my own saloon where
I could also play for the house. But I want to make the
undertaking as profitable as possible.'

Charlie was cordial once again. 'I'll let you have booze
for half the price the folks who sell the legal stuff will
charge you.'

'That's exactly what I was hoping to hear,' Hooper
looked around and then asked casually: 'I notice all of
your workers are Indians.'

'Makes good business sense,' Charlie bragged. 'White
men go into town, get drunk and talk too much. Don't
have that problem with Indians...besides...' he raised
an index finger and twirled it around taking in the five
Indians, 'Most of these redskins speak only a little English –
and hell, I think most of them don't speak any English
at all.'

Charlie Bell laughed hard at his own remark. Dehner watched the Indians' response. The anger in their eyes flared. Evidently they understood English better than their employer thought.

Hooper allowed Bell to recover from his guffaws. 'That's an excellent idea, using Indians to make the booze – was the notion yours?'

'Ah, yeh, sure.' Charlie retreated into his cigar. He looked nervous.

CHAPTER TWENTY

The sun was fully up when Dehner and Hooper approached the marshal's office and spotted the marshal and his deputy coming from the opposite direction. They exchanged good mornings as Shem unlocked the front door, and the foursome made their way inside.

'Everything OK at the schoolhouse?' Rance asked.

'Yep,' Carson answered as his deputy began to make coffee. 'Reverend Nate is in charge today. Rip and I are jus' seein' that the kids get to school and back home all right. So, how'd your visit to Charlie Bell's place go?'

Both Shem Carson and Rip Gowdy were very interested in the answer to that question. 'I had no idea Charlie was pullin' somethin' like that,' Carson said. 'His place is outta the way, never saw a reason to check on him. Reckon I should get out there and close him down.'

'I would like you to hold off on that move,' Dehner said.

'There's no hurry, our charade is safe,' Stacey added. 'I told Charlie I had enough stock to last for more than two weeks. He won't be in Conrad for ten days, so he won't learn anytime soon that I was lying to him.'

The talk stopped as Rip poured coffee and began to pass the cups around. Shem took a sip before speaking, 'No harm in waitin' a spell to arrest Charlie, I suppose, but why...'

The door was flung open and a breathless Jeremy Wilcox stormed inside. 'You gents are going to be the first to know!'

Shem Carson closed his eyes briefly; when he opened them Jeremy Wilcox was still there. The marshal's voice conveyed no enthusiasm: 'The first to know what?'

Jeremy wanted a build-up to his announcement. 'Well, as you may have noticed, I was, as always, at the school this morning, in case there was a story...'

Carson spoke in a monotone: 'Yes, Mr Wilcox, we noticed you, you tend to make it hard not to notice.'

'While there, I asked Miss Knowland if she'd like to have dinner with me,' the reporter continued, 'and she said "no".'

Rip Gowdy blew on his coffee. 'No big news there, only proves Miss Knowland's got good sense. We already knew that.'

Jeremy replied in a near shout. 'You don't understand, the reason she turned me down is, she's engaged to Reverend Nate!'

'What?!' The news obviously disturbed Rip Gowdy.

'She has consented to an interview with me,' Jeremy obviously thought his companions would be thrilled by the news of his journalistic triumph. 'She even promised to pose for a picture with Reverend Nate to go with the story. The Eastern papers are already eating up my reports on Coyote. This will add a romantic angle, and a unique one at that. Gentlemen, I'm putting Conrad on the map!'

'We're plum grateful, Mister Wilcox.'

Jeremy didn't catch the marshal's sarcasm, or chose to ignore it. 'I'm telegraphing my friend at the *New York Globe* and letting him know something big is coming his way!' The reporter scrambled out of the office.

'There oughta be a law against it,' Gowdy muttered.

Shem Carson laughed and took another sip of coffee. 'There are days when I sorta agree with you. But we got freedom of the press, and I reckon Jeremy Wilcox comes with the ranch.'

'That's not what I'm talkin' 'bout,' anger elevated Gowdy's response. 'A redskin shouldn't be marryin' a white woman. This town's been good to Reverend Nate, and he should show gratitude by actin' proper.'

Stacey cheerfully sallied into the discussion. 'Actually, marriage is considered proper conduct, as opposed to… well…I really don't think I need to elaborate.'

'But how 'bout the children…what kind of kids will they have?'

The gambler paused for a moment as if giving Gowdy's question serious thought. 'They will probably have boys and girls, that's the way these things usually work.'

Hooper's observations only caused the deputy to press his lips together in anger. The marshal tried a different approach. 'Marriage is a personal thing, Rip. We got us enough to worry 'bout. Let's jus' keep outta the private business of other folks.'

'It ain't right.' Without looking at his companions Rip Gowdy walked out of the office and slammed the door behind him.

*

Akando looked around to make sure no one was observing his movements. He then dismounted and walked over to the small half-moon rock, and lifted it off the ground. He whispered a curse at the paper that had recently been placed under the stone. But he grabbed it nonetheless and placed the rock back in place.

He didn't need much time to read the few words on the paper. He mounted and began to ride to the prearranged meeting place, trying to control the strong emotions that flamed through him.

Akando needed the white man and hated himself for it. The white man had provided him with the money for the guns. Without those guns, he could never have gotten so many young braves to follow him.

But those braves were starting to doubt him. They did not like killing wild horses before Sahale could capture them. The dead horses reminded them of the dead buffalo the white men had left to waste on the prairie.

Akando began to guide his horse up a large hill. His plan to kill the gambler had hurt him even more. He had spotted the gambler while searching for more horses to butcher with his braves. He still felt a wild anger at the man who had mocked him with his crazy smile. He had ordered an attack on the gambler, but held back himself as a chief would do.

Sahale had rescued the gambler, and two of the braves had been killed. The others had run off out of fear of the Wichita chief.

Akando rode into a grove of trees where he tied up his horse and walked toward the cave. As he ducked down and stepped inside he saw the white man sitting on a boulder drinking. The white man smiled and handed him a bottle. The white man was always generous with alcohol.

'You will no longer send me messages under a stone,' the Indian said. 'Akando will not always be looking for white man's orders he must obey. Akando is a man, not a boy who follows what others tell him.'

The white man began to laugh. His laughter echoed in the cave and seemed to surround Akando like a large, vicious creature from hell.

The white man's laughter finally stopped, and he looked with threat at his companion: 'You'll do exactly what I say…'

CHAPTER TWENTY-ONE

Rance Dehner stepped out of the marshal's office with a tin star on his shirt. The detective had often served as a volunteer deputy before in towns where he was working on a case. But this situation was different. He wasn't officially on a case. He had been dragged into the maelstrom by Stacey Hooper, for what the gambler claimed were altruistic motives.

Dehner watched his friend head for the Lucky Ace in order to, in the gambler's words, 'ply my trade'. Stacey rarely acted out of charitable motives, so why was he so interested in resolving the town's problems? Dehner could only scratch his head over that one.

And the reason for the marshal's request was also odd: 'Rance, I don't know how long it'll take my deputy to get over this snit he's in over Reverend Nate and Angie gettin' hitched, but would you mind actin' as a volunteer deputy and doin' a round?'

Dehner didn't mind, but he was concerned about Rip Gowdy. Conrad, Texas, needed the good people of the town to act in a fair and just manner in order for the town to survive. Rip Gowdy seemed to be a good man, but...

The detective continued to ponder the strange events in Conrad as he walked about the town. For a moment he tried to imagine how he would feel if he were a member of the Wichita Tribe. That notion only caused Rance to sigh in frustration. 'Seeing a situation through another man's eyes is tough, maybe impossible.'

Gunfire shattered Dehner's musings. At first he thought the shot came from the Red Eye, but a quick glance in that direction revealed people running out of Franklin's Hardware, which neighboured the saloon.

Dehner ran toward the store, drawing his gun before entering the open doorway. Inside he saw Tom Franklin standing behind a counter with his arms raised. Franklin was a man in late middle age. His muscled arms and alert eyes were a contrast to his thin grey hair and the brown spots that dotted the top of his head.

The man who stood in the middle of the store pointing a pistol at Tom was probably a year or two short of thirty, but he stood in a bent manner. His face was pale and haggard. His eyes were more red than white, and the hand that held the gun shook.

'Well, well, Rance Dehner!' The gunman's hand continued to quiver as he began to move his weapon back and forth between the store owner and the detective. 'I spotted ya in the Red Eye Saloon last Monday: remember me?'

Dehner took a step toward his adversary. 'Should I?'

The gunman's voice gained volume and intensity. 'My name's Jess Sanderson. We met three years ago in Yuma. Ya killed my brother, Carl.'

Recognition flared in Dehner's eyes. 'You and your brother were robbing an express office. I yelled for you to stop and fired a warning shot before aiming at your brother. My third shot hit you, but you still managed to get on your horse and ride. Your brother was wounded, but kept firing and put up a tough fight. Carl died to save you from a jail cell.'

'That's right, and now I'm gonna get revenge. I'm gonna kill you.' Sanderson pulled back the hammer on his pistol and pointed it at Franklin. 'Holster that Colt, Dehner, or I kill the counter jumper.'

Rance holstered his gun. Sanderson's smile reflected a grotesque satisfaction. 'This ain't jus' revenge for my brother. Ya shot me in the leg that day and I ain't been able to walk right since. Ya not only killed my brother, ya ruined my life.'

'You crazy little man!' the shout came from behind the counter.

Jess Sanderson shouted back. 'Don't ya call me a little man!'

'I'll call you anything I want,' Tom Franklin lowered his arms as if showing he didn't fear the intruder. 'Any man who goes 'round feelin' sorry for himself is little. I fought in the war between the states. Came out of it with a piece of wood for half of my right leg. Never felt sorry for myself and never had reason to – I've done ever'thing I set out to do.'

Sanderson screamed obscenities at the store owner, turning away from Dehner for a moment. Rance lurched at the gunman, knocked the weapon out of his hand and then downed him with a hard right punch.

'Do you want to bring charges against this saddle bum, Tom?'

Franklin shrugged his shoulders. 'Naa, but you might. I don't mean sour apples to Sandy or whatever the scalawag's name is, he jus' wanted to git you in here. If your trails cross ag'in, he might try to backshoot ya.'

Dehner nodded at the weapon lying on the floor. 'I'll leave that in your hands.' He grabbed the would-be killer by the scruff of his neck and walked him to the boardwalk outside the store.

'Where's your horse?' Dehner's voice made the question a demand.

Sanderson pointed to a sorrel tied up at a nearby hitch rail. Rance pushed him twice in that direction. The second push almost caused Sanderson to collide with his steed.

Dehner pointed an accusing finger at the man who had tried to kill him. 'You get on your horse and ride, never let me see you in this town again. In fact, I'd better never see you again, anywhere. Ride!'

Sanderson mounted slowly, as he always did because of his bad leg. His head was still woozy from the punch, which also slowed his movements. Dehner watched as the man began to ride out of town. Then Sanderson suddenly turned around and shouted what sounded like a threat to the detective. The words came out in a muffled manner, and Sanderson immediately followed it up by spurring his sorrel into a fast gallop out of town.

Rance watched the dust cloud dissipate and wondered why he had let a man who had vowed to kill him go free. He looked at the fleeing saddle bum who was now a vanishing speck, and spoke quietly to himself, 'Sanderson is more pathetic than dangerous, there was no need…'

A pleasant smile suddenly ran across the detective's face. He had let the saddle bum go in order to please Beth Page.

Many of Dehner's memories of Beth were torturous. She had died in the cross-fire when she ran into the midst of a gunfight he was involved in as a deputy sheriff. But before that horror occurred they had enjoyed such wonderful moments together.

The detective used an index finger to push his hat back. Beth had a very special but crazy way of looking at things. She would have hated Jess Sanderson for trying to kill the man she loved. At the same time she would have felt sorry for Sanderson because he had to go through life with a bad leg: a bad leg that came with the compliments of Rance Dehner.

Dehner's smile broadened. This was one of the times when the memory of Beth Page made him feel good. Rance Dehner turned and continued to do his round.

CHAPTER TWENTY-TWO

Howard Dixon stood in the room that had once belonged to Sam. The word 'Coyote' still dominated one wall. 'Looks like the devil himself put it there with his branding iron.'

The new owner of the Red Eye was speaking to two gunmen he had just hired. One was a tall, heavyset man a few years on the far side of forty named Jonas. The other was a few years short of twenty, with an average height and build, named Billy. Dixon had forgotten their last names.

Billy spoke up in the over-confident style of youth. 'I hear the person who put that there is a detective from…'

'That's a lie told by the law,' Dixon snapped. 'One thing you gotta learn fast is never to trust the law!'

'Right! You can bet I'll never forgit that, not ever!'

Jonas gave a slight smile at his pard's desire to please. Still, the kid had been a real help since he had seen him showing off his skills with a gun at a small town picnic. The aging gun for hire had convinced the young man that an exciting life lay ahead for the partner of Jonas Krammer. A month later the kid still believed it.

'Let me go over what is expected of you gents,' Howard stuck his thumbs into his belt, hoping the pose made him look tough. 'For the time bein' you'll both work the Red Eye at nights. You'll look after the main floor downstairs and the business goin' on up here. No funny stuff with the gals, I ain't payin' you to pleasure yourselves.'

Billy nodded his head vigorously and appeared anxious to hear the rest of the orders. Jonas's face remained a blank slate.

'One of you will stay here all night in case some jasper gives the girls a hard time,' Dixon continued. 'The other needs to be here in the afternoons. I'll let you gents work that out yourselfs. Now, get downstairs. I'll be down shortly after I get some work done.'

After the gunmen departed, Dixon looked at the desk that had belonged to Sam only two days ago. He needed to go through her records, but was too restless to do it on this night.

His eyes shifted back to the writing on the wall, and his body trembled even though the night was hot. Since childhood he had been afraid of monsters. Unlike his playmates, he hated stories about ghosts and dragons. Now there seemed to be a real monster stalking the town.

Howard had little confidence in his two new hires, but they were cheap and would have to do for the time being. He had more expensive gunnies working at the Lucky Ace where he kept his main office and where he slept.

The saloon owner forced a smile on his face as he walked down the stairway of the Red Eye. Only a small scattering of customers were rattling about the main floor, but that didn't bother Howard Dixon. It was early in the evening.

Vince Bursey was leaning against the bar nursing a beer. One side of his head was still blue and swollen from having Rance Dehner's gun smash against it during the attempt to block Indian kids from the school. Howard approached Bursey in a robust, friendly manner. Bursey had been mad at him for not drawing a gun during the mêlée at the school.

Howard scooted behind the bar and pointed at the mug in front of Vince. 'Harry, this beer is on the house, and so is the next one for Vince Bursey. We're honored to have one of Conrad's finest citizens patronizing us on the Red Eye's first night under new ownership!'

'Yes sir!' Harry grabbed a coin from under the counter and tossed it to Vince. 'There's your money back. Let me know when ya need a refill.'

Vince caught the coin, thanked the bar keep, and then turned to Howard. 'Looks like you're gettin' off to a good start.'

'Thanks, and tonight will not be the only time there will be drinks on the house.'

Dixon's promise of free drinks seemed to diminish Bursey's anger toward him. The saddle shop owner glanced at the bar keep who was now out of hearing range, then spoke in a low voice. 'Have you heard 'bout what that damned redskin is pullin' now?'

'Which redskin?'

'That preacher man, Nate: he's marryin' Angie Knowland!'

The shock on Dixon's face was genuine. 'What?!'

Bursey's speech turned guttural. 'Yep, that Injun will soon be takin' the prettiest gal in town into his tepee. What d'you think of that?'

'I think...'

Dixon stopped talking as Sahale stepped into the Red Eye. The Indian nodded at Harry as he approached the bar and laid down some money, 'A beer please.'

The barkeep waved a friendly greeting. 'Things have changed 'round this place.'

'Yes,' Sahale replied. 'I saw Sam and Lafe a few times when I came by, but had never spoken to them. I am told they tried to do some terrible things.'

'Yep,' Harry tried to lighten the mood as he placed a mug in front of his customer. 'But the Red Eye still serves the coldest beer in town, jus' the way ya like it.'

Sahale smiled his appreciation as he took a sip of the brew. Harry leaned against the bar. 'So, ya gonna be in town long, Sahale?'

'I shall be leaving at sunrise. I have just been talking with my good friend, Nata... Reverend Nate. I wanted to congratulate him.'

'He's a lucky guy,' Harry responded with enthusiasm. 'Angie Knowland is a great gal, and what a looker...'

Howard Dixon was surprised by the cordial friendship between Harry and Sahale. Normally the situation would bother him, but on this night he could put it to good use.

Dixon gave Vince Bursey a heads-up glance, then strolled from behind the bar to a table where Jonas and Billy were fussing with a deck of cards and looking bored. Their boss talked to them for several minutes, and they didn't look bored any longer.

Billy got up from the table and walked too casually to the bar. As far as Dixon could tell, Sahale didn't take much notice of the kid. Still, the saloon owner tensed up, afraid the boy couldn't play the role he had been assigned.

'Please bring me a beer, barkeep,' Billy spoke as he slapped both hands on the bar.

Harry guffawed loudly. 'Don't have many customers who say "please", guess I should oblige ya right quick.'

'Thanks!' Billy turned to the other man standing at the bar. 'Some saloons I go to, they hooraw me …say I should be drinkin' milk!'

Sahale had been enjoying his beer and his talk with Harry, and was now amused by the boy standing near him. He had allowed himself to relax, and didn't notice the pudgy middle-aged man who was getting up from a table and walking in his direction.

'I'm glad you enjoy the service here. Harry is an excellent bartender,' the Indian said.

Billy picked up the mug which had just been placed in front of him and raised it as if in a toast, 'To your health.'

Sahale smiled and raised his mug in kind.

'Say, ain't you a Wichita?' Billy asked after placing his mug down.

'Yes, you are correct.'

'I didn't know the Wichita were even in Texas,' the boy said.

'The Wichita are not plentiful in this part of the country,' Sahale began to explain. 'You will find…'

A massive explosion slammed a red wall against Sahale's eyes. He fought for consciousness as he dropped to the floor, inwardly cursing himself for being so careless. As his vision returned he realized that he was face down on the floor. Instinctively he tried to get up, another mistake. This time a black wall hit him and his body splayed limp against the splintered, rough wood.

CHAPTER TWENTY-THREE

'What the hell!' Harry shouted.

'Shut up!' Dixon, who had been standing back, now ran toward the bar.

Vince Bursey was crouched over Sahale. 'The Injun's out cold.'

Howard Dixon looked at the few customers who were scattered across the saloon, and shouted: 'No problem, gents, we jus' got a redskin here who didn't wanna pay for his drinks. Go ahead and enjoy yourselfs while we put out the trash.'

The Red Eye patrons laughed a bit and gladly followed Howard's advice. Jonas stood over the Indian, gun in hand, as if the man he had just assaulted was still a serious threat.

Vince lifted himself out of the crouch. 'What ya gonna do?'

Harry's face was ashen. 'I don't unnerstand —'

Howard pointed a threatening finger at his bartender. 'I told you to shut up!' Dixon switched his glance to Bursey. 'A couple days ago, you thought I wasn't tough enough. Well, tonight we're gettin' tough.'

Bursey caught the challenge in Dixon's statement. He paused a moment then proclaimed, 'I'm in.'

Jonas spoke as he holstered his pistol. 'Whatcha got in mind?'

Howard pointed at a door to the right of the bar between the bar and the staircase. 'Let's take him in there.'

Dixon, Bursey and the two hired guns lifted Sahale and carried him into the stock room where they laid him on the floor. 'Tie him up,' Dixon ordered his gunnies.

Jonas had worked for fools before and wasn't about to say 'yes sir' to this jasper. 'We'll be needin' a rope to do that.'

Billy, believing the promised excitement had at last arrived, was anxious to please. 'My horse is tied up right outside. I'll get the rope from my saddle.' He ran off on his mission.

'OK, we tie the Injun up,' Jonas sounded frustrated and angry. 'Then what?! You seem to be avoidin' that question, boss man.'

Howard paused, and for a moment his lips trembled, though he said nothing. Jonas was right, he hadn't thought this through. He had seen that damned Indian standing in *his* saloon talking to *his* bartender about another Indian marrying a white woman. He couldn't stand for that!

Vince, who had been on his side moments ago, now gave him a questioning stare. The saloon owner knew what Vince was thinking. Howard Dixon had failed to draw his gun two days ago when the chips were down. Was he a coward?

The door banged open and Billy scampered in holding a rope up high like a fisherman proudly displaying his catch. The smile vanished from the kid's face as he caught the tension in the room.

Howard's words were low and uncertain. 'We're goin' to hang the redskin.'

Vince's eyes rounded. 'Sahale's a chief!'

The anger in Jonas's voice intensified. 'Look, boss man, you hired us to look after your damned saloon, not to hang some chief and set off Injun trouble!'

But Howard had stepped over a line and couldn't go back. 'You'll do what I tell you!'

'You're jawin' 'bout a dangerous job, boss man!' Jonas waved a thumb at Billy. 'We'll need one hunnert dollars a-piece, now!'

A low moaning sound came from the floor. Dixon looked at Billy, whom he thought was more open to obeying orders. 'You got your rope, tie the redskin up!'

Jonas held up a palm in the kid's direction. 'We don't do nothin' 'till we get our money.'

Howard smirked as if two hundred dollars was a small thing to him. 'I gotta get a buckboard anyhows. We'll need it to get Sahale outta town and to a nice cottonwood. I'll get your money, now tie up the redskin.'

'OK, boss man, but we ain't leavin' town 'till we get paid.' Jonas untied his bandanna and then crouched over Sahale and began to gag him with it.

Billy got down on one knee and began to wrap the rope around Sahale's ankles. The kid was usually good with a rope, but now his hands quivered and he had to work slowly. Billy wanted to be back at that small town picnic. He never thought the excitement Jonas talked about would involve hanging a man who hadn't been accused of a crime, never mind found guilty of anything. He had wanted to be a gunfighter.

Don't worry none. That's what Billy had written in the note he had left for his parents. But he knew they were worried, his ma probably cried every day...

Billy wiped the moisture from his own eyes and a terrible dread came over him. He was about to take part in a hanging. The way the law looked at it, that was just like killing a man. His life would never be the same: he was about to become an outlaw wanted for murder.

*

Rance Dehner and a sullen Rip Gowdy were planning on how to do the rounds for that evening when Harry Foster entered the office, breathing hard.

'What's up, Harry?' Gowdy responded to the frantic expression on the bartender's face.

'That fool Howard Dixon and a few other jaspers have knocked Sahale out cold. They tied him up and got him on the bed of a buckboard with a tarp over him. They're ridin' outta town somewhere. They're gonna hang him!'

'How many of them are there?' Dehner asked.

'Four: Dixon, Vince Bursey and two hardcases Dixon just put on the payroll.'

The detective snapped another question. 'Have they left yet?'

'Yep. They pulled out a few minutes ago, heading north.' Harry's top lip raised over his teeth as if he were snarling. 'Dixon told me that if I went to the law, he'd fire me... well, to hell with him!'

'That may be where he ends up tonight. Thanks, Harry.' Dehner turned to the deputy. 'Let's go!'

CHAPTER
TWENTY-FOUR

Rip Gowdy and Dehner stood behind the Red Eye Saloon examining recent tracks from a buckboard. 'We have a bright moon to work with tonight,' Dehner said. 'Those tracks are pretty deep, they're using a heavy wagon. That will help us.'

'Howard Dixon will help us even more.'

Dehner gave his companion a quizzical look.

'Dixon is a braggart, but he ain't got that much to brag about,' Gowdy explained. 'He'll give the orders, but he don't know the area all that good. Harry said he headed north.' The deputy nodded at the ground. 'This little road runs north then connects with a trail that goes northeast. Lots of trees that way, and ever'one knows it. Howard will take that trail 'cause he don't know to do anythin' different.'

Both men mounted their horses and rode at a fast lope, pausing only briefly at the northeast trail. 'You were right,' Dehner declared. They began to ride at a fast gallop.

In less than fifteen minutes, Rance held up a hand, indicating they should stop. 'Listen carefully,' the detective whispered to Rip.

'Sounds like a buckboard pullin' up,' Gowdy said.

Dehner let out a low breath of frustration. 'We were riding too fast. They heard us coming.'

'Whatcha think we should do?'

Dehner glanced at the woods beside him. 'There's plenty of distance between those trees.'

'Yeh,' Rip agreed. Like Dehner he spoke in a whisper. 'They're probably pulling the wagon into the woods and settin' up an ambush.'

'We'll let the horses go without us.'

Rance's suggestion seemed to amuse the deputy. 'Maybe we can pull a little surprise of our own.'

After dismounting, the two men pulled Winchesters from their scabbards and slapped the horses. Both steeds moved ahead at a casual pace. Dehner hastily removed his boots and motioned for the deputy to do the same.

As they entered the woods, Gowdy understood Rance's instructions. They needed to move quickly and sock feet softened their steps.

Before the two men were in sight of their targets, they could hear Vince Bursey's voice snap, 'Here they come!'

A tense silence followed as four men prepared to send a fusillade of bullets at the approaching riders. Howard Dixon's voice broke the silence with a loud, 'Damn! Those horses are riderless. What the...'

An intense whisper cut him off. Someone was no doubt telling the saloon owner to shut up. He was giving away their location.

The advice came too late. Dehner and Gowdy could now see a buckboard arranged so that the broad side faced the road and could be a shield against any bullets coming from it. Four men were crouched behind the wagon. Two horses were attached to the buckboard. Three other horses were nearby, nibbling leaves from the surrounding trees.

'Throw down your guns and lift your hands, all of you, now!'

A red flash followed Dehner's order. The detective dropped to the ground and fired his rifle. A horrible child-like scream cut through the darkness. Dehner and Gowdy watched as a shadow dropped his pistol and then clung to the buckboard. A wavering voice began to beseech Jesus in a desperate prayer. A loud gasp ended the prayer and the shadow plunged to the dirt.

Dehner jumped back on to his feet. He and Gowdy took several steps toward the would-be bushwackers. 'Drop your guns and lift those hands,' the detective yelled. 'I won't say it again.'

The order was aimed at Vince Bursey and a heavy-set man Dehner didn't recognize. Howard Dixon already had his arms in the air.

Bursey's body began to tremble. The store owner appeared to be working up the courage to fire.

He never got the chance. The figure of Sahale emerged from under the tarp and jumped on to the shop owner. As both men went down, the Indian grabbed Bursey's gun. Sahale held tight to the weapon as he rolled a few feet away from his adversary.

'We will now both get up very slowly,' Sahale spoke in a firm monotone. But the Indian's body wobbled as he stood up. The rope had hindered the circulation to his feet.

Dehner and Rip Gowdy moved quickly toward the buckboard. Dehner's eyes remained on the stranger. 'Drop the gun, mister!'

Jonas dropped his weapon and raised his hands.

Gowdy stepped quickly toward Sahale. 'You OK?'

'Yes,' the Indian replied, 'but it took me longer to get free of the rope than it should have.'

For a few moments, Dehner peered at the wound on Sahale's head: a few moments too long. When he looked back, Jonas was preparing to mount one of the horses. The gunslick had moved with surprising silence and speed for such a bulky man.

Rance grabbed the deputy's arm as Rip was about to fire on the fleeing gun for hire. 'We may be able to get some valuable information from that buzzard.' Dehner's eyes shifted between Rip and Sahale, as he handed Sahale the Winchester he had been using. 'Can you two keep an eye on things here?'

Both men gave a fast nod as Jonas rode out of the woods and on to the trail. Dehner ran toward the two remaining free horses and mounted what appeared to be the stronger one. As his foot hit the stirrup, the detective remembered he was in sock feet.

'I'm depending on your good will,' Rance said to the buckskin.

The detective guided the horse on to the trail and kneed him into a fast run. The buckskin made good time and was soon within sight of the escaping gunman. Jonas heard the hoofbeats behind him and cursed his bad luck. He had not grabbed the fastest horse.

Maybe he could fix that. One well placed bullet could bring down the horse behind him and maybe cripple his pursuer. Jonas pulled out the small derringer pocketed in his gun belt.

The shot missed by several feet. Then Jonas suddenly screamed in pain. His body jerked violently as he was thrown back and hit the trail hard.

Dehner pulled up his horse and considered the situation as well as the moonlight would permit. He dismounted and, gun in hand, cautiously approached the form that lay on the ground.

The caution was unnecessary. As he got closer to the body, Dehner realized what had happened. A large branch hung over the trail from a tree to one side of it. The gunny's attention had been totally on making a good shot, and he had paid no attention to what was directly in front of him.

Rance bent over the lifeless form, and had his suspicions confirmed. The outlaw's skull was crushed. If the man had any valuable information to give, no one would ever hear it.

The detective retrieved the outlaw's horse and tied his corpse over the saddle. The steed may not have been fast, but the smell of blood didn't seem to bother him.

Whinnies sounded from nearby. Rance mounted and, holding the reins of the outlaw's horse, rode further down the road to where he found the horses that he and Rip Gowdy had employed as decoys. They were both contentedly nibbling bits of tall grass, unaware of, or indifferent to, all of the human violence that had ravaged the peacefulness of night. Dehner watched the two steeds for a moment as if they were conveying a deeper truth, a truth he couldn't comprehend.

The detective suddenly shook his head as if coming out of a deep sleep. He tied the reins of the two horses to that of the horse carrying the dead outlaw, turned, and began to ride back to the reality that awaited him. 'I'll contemplate nature on the day when I finally get to go fishing,' Dehner whispered to himself.

Arriving back at the buckboard, Rance dismounted and saw that another steed also carried a gruesome cargo. Rip and Sahale had tied the man Rance had fired on and killed across the horse's saddle. Rance Dehner paused, and then did what he had to do: he carefully examined the dead gunman, including a look at his face.

'Oh no,' the detective closed his eyes for a moment before walking toward the buckboard where Rip and Sahale were waiting. 'He was only a kid, couldn't have been more than seventeen.'

Sahale placed a hand on Rance's shoulder. 'Rip told me all that happened. When a man is firing at you there are no alternatives.'

Dehner nodded his head as he pointed at the bed of the buckboard where Vince Bursey and Howard Dixon were sitting beside each other with their hands and feet tied. 'Both gents got off easy after trying to keep Indian children out of school; too bad they didn't learn any lesson from it. I don't think Vince and Howard will be as good at breaking loose from ropes as you are, Sahale.'

'This is outrageous!' Howard Dixon shouted. 'I'm a respectable businessman. You've got no right to treat me like some common crook!'

'This was all your idea, Dixon!' Bursey glared at his accomplice. 'I ain't takin' no fault for what you done!'

The exchange pleased Dehner. The two men were already turning on each other. They would end up in competition to see whose testimony would condemn the other to the longest prison sentence.

'We'll jus' see how respectable ya two buzzards look in a damned jail cell.' The anger in Rip's voice surprised his two companions.

Responding to that anger, Dehner spoke in a soft manner. 'Sahale, could you drive the wagon? I'll ride behind. Rip can ride beside you.'

'I will drive slowly at first, so that I will know when to stop.' Sahale responded.

Dehner gave the chief a questioning look.

Sahale smiled as he pointed downwards. 'We very much need to stop and pick up your boots. Both you and Deputy Gowdy must be getting sore feet.'

CHAPTER
TWENTY-FIVE

Reverend Nate smiled at his fiancée. 'We are doing the right thing,' he quietly assured her.

Angie Knowland returned the smile, but it was fragile: 'I wish the right thing didn't make me so nervous.'

Something fine passed between them, then the pastor turned to face the small assemblage. Reverend Nate and Angie were standing in front of the platform of the Conrad Community Church, looking at a gathering of seven people sitting in the front pews only a few feet away from them. 'Angie and I want to thank all of you for coming here this afternoon.'

Nate looked directly at his long-time friend. 'Sahale, I'm glad you were not seriously injured last night.'

The Wichita chief shrugged his shoulders in a comical manner. 'Perhaps I should follow the advice of some of the more exuberant members of your profession and stay out of saloons.'

Nate laughed along with the others, but that couldn't cover his edginess. He clasped his hands together to cover the fact that they were quivering. 'As all of you know, I am a very blessed man. Miss Angie Knowland has agreed to be my wife.'

Applause and cheers emanated from the seven men. Nate smiled and continued: 'Angie and I have decided to be married here immediately after the service this Sunday. We've already made arrangements. A friend of mine, Reverend Paul Ambler, will be arriving tomorrow. He will do the service. His wife will be playing the piano. Everyone in Conrad is invited!'

Shem Carson's voice rose immediately. 'That's a dangerous notion, Preacher! Akando's ultimatum ends on Monday morning! He's made all sorts of threats, and then there's all this Coyote stuff goin' on. Preacher, your weddin' would be a perfect target for Akando and whoever is behind this Coyote business. Please, postpone it 'till ever'thing gets settled!'

Angie spoke softly as she looked at the marshal. 'It is precisely *because of* Akando, Coyote and "all this stuff" that we are having the wedding this Sunday.'

'I don't follow you,' the lawman admitted.

'So much of the violence and hatred that has been eating at this town isn't connected to Akando or Coyote,' Angie explained. 'Not directly, anyhow. Coyote has just been the match that set off the explosion. Think about it – Sam kidnapped me and my father, and two people ended up dead. Last night, Howard Dixon and Vince Bursey tried to hang Sahale. Coyote had nothing to do with any of that. It was all about greed and hate. What this town needs is an opportunity for the many decent people to come together and express their goodwill. Nate and I are going to give them that chance this Sunday.'

Shem Carson's face reflected some agreement with what the young woman had just said. Still, he looked troubled.

Nate spoke up quickly, sensing that his fiancée's words had made a strong impact. 'We need the help of you gentlemen to make this work. He looked at his future father-in-law. 'Dade, we appreciate…'

Dade Knowland waved a hand as if telling Reverend Nate to move on: 'My daughter has already persuaded me!'

Nate continued, 'Sahale, you are to be my best man, so you'll be an easy target for anyone bent on trouble.'

'I am honored to be your best man, Nate, and as chief of the Wichita I will come appropriately dressed.'

Nate smiled broadly and then looked at Conrad's one journalist. 'Jeremy, if you could have a story about our wedding in the paper on Saturday it would be a big help in getting the word out.'

'Happy to oblige, Reverend,' Wilcox proclaimed. 'You and Miss Knowland make great copy – why, I'll…'

An exasperated Shem Carson cut him off: 'You'll get the story in the New York newspapers, congratulations Mr Wilcox!'

Nate looked directly at the four men who were sitting side by side. He knew they required his hardest sale. 'Shem, Rip, Stacey and Rance, I know the wedding will cause the most trouble for you gentlemen. You will be seeing that everyone is safe. Angie and I deeply appreciate all of you, and thank you. I hope you understand why we think it is important to do the wedding this way.'

'I unnerstand, Preacher, and I sorta see your point,' Shem's voice was now pleading. 'But this idea of yours, I mean it's fine and ever'thing, but it's jus' too…' the marshal paused, realizing he was in a church and a lady was present, 'it's jus' too darned dangerous.'

Rip Gowdy suddenly stood up from the pew and approached the couple. He stood facing them. 'Miss Knowland, Reverent, I owe ya both an apology.'

Nate's mouth twisted in surprise. 'You don't owe us a thing, Rip.'

The deputy replied firmly. 'Yes, I do. When I heard 'bout you two gettin' hitched I tole anyone who was fool enough ta listen ta me that it weren't right for a white woman to marry an Indian. And the words I sometimes used weren't decent.'

Gowdy looked down at the floor and then once again faced the couple. 'Well, last night Rance Dehner and me stopped two so-called respectable citizens and their hired gunnies from hangin' Sahale. Sahale is a fine man, and the people who tried to kill him are nothin' but lowlifes. Because of those lowlifes a kid who weren't much more than seventeen is dead. Ever'one jus' called him Billy. Nobody even knowed his last name. We buried him this mornin'. His folks may never know what became of their boy.'

Rip fell silent and his face began to contort. Nate placed a hand on the deputy's shoulder. When Rip Gowdy spoke again his voice quivered. 'I reckon Billy was like me at that age, lookin' for excitement and wantin' ta prove he was a man. Well, thanks to those two fine citizens, Howard Dixon and Vince Bursey, Billy will never get ta be a man.'

Rip Gowdy inhaled deeply and his voice steadied. 'Reverent Nate, Miss Knowland, I'll be honored to help out anyways I can with your weddin'.'

Nate shook hands with Rip, and then Angie gave the deputy a gentle hug. Stacey Hooper spoke in a loud whisper to his companions. 'Well, gentlemen, it appears that we need to get busy with wedding preparations.'

CHAPTER TWENTY-SIX

Charlie Bell gave a caustic smile as he sat in Ma Trent's restaurant, reading the *Conrad Gazette* and finishing his lunch. So, Reverend Nate and that pretty schoolmarm were getting hitched tomorrow, and the whole town was invited to the ceremony. He guessed that accounted for the festive air he had noticed when he arrived in Conrad an hour or so ago.

Charlie rarely came into town. 'Out of sight, out of mind,' he whispered to himself, thinking primarily of the town's marshal. 'But a man needs a decent meal and a chance to pleasure himself now and ag'in.'

The moonshiner finished his apple pie, paid for the eats, and then did a casual stroll to Knowland's General Store. There was a boisterous crowd inside squawking about the wedding the next day. Few people noticed Charlie as he bought some rock candy, two dime novels and an issue of the *Police Gazette*. All of the items, along with the newspaper he had purchased at the restaurant, would bring him some enjoyment later on.

'Time for some serious enjoyment right now,' Charlie's isolation had long ago gotten him into the habit of talking to himself.

He walked outside the store, stopped, and took in the bright sun and the bustle. He wondered which saloon to patronize. 'The Red Eye, of course. Stacey Hooper is high hat, bet his gals are first class.'

Bell placed the candy in his coat pocket and took his time walking to the saloon. As he stepped through the bat wings his eyes skimmed over the female flesh in their flashy dresses who dotted the Red Eye. But his first stop was at the bar, where Harry was attending to customers.

'A beer please,' Charlie dropped a coin on the mahogany as he ordered. 'Is the boss around?'

Harry looked confused. The moonshiner waved his hand, indicating that the question was not important. 'Never mind, I'm in town for pleasure, business can wait for another day.'

Beer in hand, he strolled to an empty table and sat down, placing the dime novels, magazine and paper in front of him. He had just taken the third sip of his beer when a feminine voice purred, 'Can I join you, or would I get in the way of your reading?'

She was attractive, and still young enough that the despair of a prostitute's life didn't reflect in her face: not too much, anyway. Besides, Charlie wasn't in a fussy mood.

Bell nodded at the reading material. 'These are for later. I pretty much live alone.'

'Ahhh!' The woman replied in mock sympathy. 'Well, you don't have to be alone now.'

There was a routine here that Charlie Bell wanted to get out of the way as quickly as possible, 'What's your name, honey?'

The woman laughed playfully. 'My name is Honey!'

Bell threw his head back and made a loud laugh, pretending he found the situation to be hilarious. 'Well, sit down Honey and I'll buy you a drink.'

Twenty minutes and a lot of false laughter later, Honey moved matters to where she knew her companion wanted them to go. 'You look tired, Charlie, would you like to come upstairs and relax a bit before heading home? She scooped up the reading material on the table. 'Harry will keep these under the bar for you.'

'Sure Honey, I'll bet you could make me feel right comfortable.'

Charlie Bell put his arm around the woman's waist as they made their way up the stairs to the second floor. Stopping at the third room, Honey broke away from her companion and gave him a wink as she opened the door and motioned him inside.

As Charlie stepped into the room, Honey slammed the door behind him. The moonshiner was alone. 'What the...'

Charlie Bell yelled in pain as his arm was pinned behind him and he was pushed face first on to a bed. A familiar voice demanded: 'What the hell are you doing here?!'

Bell's reply was muffled by the mattress. 'I just came into town for a little...'

'You stay out of town until I tell you different. Do you want to ruin everything?!'

'I only...'

'Leave now, and leave quick!' Charlie was lifted off the bed, walked to the door and pushed outside.

For a moment, Bell stood in the hall rubbing his sore arm. His eyes looked over the floor below him. He didn't see Honey. 'Who cares about a stupid whore? I never want to lay eyes on her ag'in.'

Charlie realized the urgency of heeding the warning he had just been given. He moved down the stairs quickly and headed for the bat wings.

'Mister!'

The voice hit him like a shot. The moonshiner's shoulders lifted in stunned surprise.

Harry stepped out from behind the bar and handed Charlie four items. 'These belong to you, mister. Happy reading!'

Charlie ran out of the Red Eye, mounted his horse and galloped out of town.

CHAPTER TWENTY-SEVEN

Akando hastily brushed the perspiration off his forehead. Sweat had dribbled into his eyes, stinging them and blurring his vision.

The sun was blistering hot despite the fact that it was only mid-morning. Akando mused to himself about what was now happening in town. At the Conrad Community Church Nata would be just beginning the service, confident that his wedding was only a few hours away. The man who now called himself Reverend Nate didn't have the slightest notion that his wedding would have to proceed without a best man.

Akando fidgeted as he looked out from behind a cottonwood at the trail which ran along the thick line of trees. Sahale would appear soon. As most members of the Wichita tribe did when they rode into town on a hot day, Sahale would stop here, leave the trail, and allow his horse to drink at the river that ran alongside the trees.

The renegade caressed the large knife that lay against his right thigh. The white man had ordered him to kill Sahale with the knife. He could use the rifle in his hands to hold the Wichita chief prisoner, but there must be no bullets found in Sahale's body. The white man's instructions had been specific.

Sahale's death must look like the work of Coyote. This will be Coyote's biggest kill. After Sahale is gone we will bring back the monster when and if we need him.

Akando's anger with the white man was diminishing. The white man was wise in his own way.

We've lucked out! This wedding has changed everything. The law thinks there's going to be big trouble at the ceremony. They will all be on guard at the church. Sahale will be riding alone.

Hoofbeats intruded on Akando's thoughts. He watched Sahale approach on his fine chestnut. The chief was wearing the large headdress he only used for special occasions.

The renegade made an ugly grin. Yes, today would be a special occasion. He had been wanting to kill Sahale for a long time.

The chestnut had made this ride often and needed little prodding to turn where there was a large space between the trees. Repeated use of the area had created a path to the river.

Sahale dismounted at the water and patted his horse as it drank. His back remained to Akando.

The renegade moved quickly but quietly to his enemy and poked the barrel of the Winchester into his back. 'Sahale will spend the last moments of his life taking orders from Akando.'

'As you say,' came the reply.

'For once in his life, Sahale is showing wisdom as he bows to the power of Akando.' The renegade pulled his knife from the sheath. 'Akando has already killed a worthless drunk and a homesteader who thought he could stop me with a gun. Now will come my biggest kill.'

'Akando talks much about his power, and yet he is the puppet of a white man.'

The renegade froze for a moment. The words were those of Sahale, but they didn't come from the man in front of him. Akando turned his head back toward the trees where the Wichita chief was walking toward him. 'You have killed for a white man,' Sahale said. 'Now you must face the white man's justice.'

Another voice sounded from out of the trees. 'Drop the gun and the knife, Akando, now!'

The renegade's mind spun in frantic confusion. The spin became more intense as he turned back to the man wearing a headdress.

Stacey Hooper beamed a contented smile. 'I now have an even deeper respect for your chief. I don't know how he manages with this headdress. I must confess that it gives me a headache.'

Akando held a Winchester in one hand and a knife in the other, but remained confused as to how to use them. A voice behind him repeated the order. 'Drop the weapons, Akando, this is your last chance.'

Dehner's words 'last chance' struck the renegade hard. In a panicked move, he swung the knife at Stacey Hooper who jumped back and then lunged forward, landing a kick to the Indian's knee.

Akando dropped the knife. Stacey smashed a fist into the Indian's eye. Akando staggered backwards and swung the Winchester at the gambler. But the swing was weak. The gun hit Stacey on the shoulder and then did a fast descent to the ground. Hooper tried to quickly scoop up the Winchester, but Akando clasped both hands together and made them a weapon he brought down hard on Stacey's neck. The gambler dropped on to the rifle.

As Rance Dehner and Sahale ran toward him, Akando mounted Sahale's horse. The chestnut began to buck. Akando prodded the steed a few steps into the river but he was still groggy from Stacey's assault. The animal threw him off.

Dehner tossed his Colt on to the ground and ran into the river, taking care to avoid a collision with the chestnut, which was returning to shore. He was waist deep in water when he caught up with Akando and landed a hard right jab, which made a crunching sound on the renegade's nose.

The detective then pulled his adversary through the water and dropped him at Sahale's feet. Rance helped Stacey up and both men were quickly mesmerized by the look on the Wichita chief's face. Was it pity, anger, regret over some lost opportunity, or something else? Neither man could even guess at an answer.

Sahale's eyes remained fixed on the man who now lay on the ground moaning through the cupped hands that covered his face. 'You tried to prove yourself a leader by slaughtering horses. Then you killed a helpless drunk and an innocent homesteader who only wished to provide well for his family. You are unworthy, Akando. You will die by a rope and be buried where the white man chooses to bury you.'

Akando kept his hands over his face. The sounds of his moans changed. The man may have been crying.

Rance spoke softly to the figure on the ground, trying to take advantage of the situation. 'Sahale is right. You're going to hang. But you could gain some honour back by telling us everything that has happened, including the name of the person you have been working with in this Coyote scheme.'

Angry, frantic words came from Akando.

'A good effort, Rance,' Stacey said. 'But I'm afraid our defeated foe is staying in character.'

'Guess so,' Rance glanced over his wet clothes. 'The sun should have me dry in less than an hour. Stacey, you need to give Sahale his clothes back, and make it fast. We don't want to be late for the wedding.'

CHAPTER TWENTY-EIGHT

Angie Knowland walked down the aisle of the church on her father's arm. This was nothing like her dream. Nate was watching her, but he wasn't standing on the platform. That position was taken by Reverend Ambler, whose wife, June, was at the piano playing the bridal march.

Angie was not wearing a gown ordered from a catalogue. There had been no time for that. But her father had given her the best dress available at Knowland's General Store. She had spent hours and lost sleep altering the dress to make it appear more like a bridal gown. When she had put the dress on this morning, she realized the hours and effort made the dress special in a way that could never be matched by something that arrived in the mail.

And, unlike the dream, the church was not covered in flowers. But there were a few vases of flowers at the front which had been beautifully arranged by Madelynn Taylor. Angie was certain those flowers wouldn't wilt during the ceremony.

The young woman arrived at the front. Her father took a step back and Nate smiled lovingly at her. This wasn't like the dream, this was a lot better!

As Reverend Ambler began to speak, another thought occurred to the bride. Rance Dehner had added an additional feature to their nuptials. How many weddings are used as part of a plan to capture a killer? No doubt about it, she would have a great story to share with her children.

*

'Say cheese!' Jeremy Wilcox shouted moments before he took a picture of the newly married couple standing outside the church.

Cheers followed after Jeremy worked his magic with the brown wooden object that perched on a tripod. Reverend Nate spoke as the noise subsided. 'Thank you, Jeremy, and thanks to all of you for sharing this wonderful day with Angie and me.'

A shout came from one of the hundred or so people gathered there. 'Ya shoulda said, "my wife and me", Preacher!'

Reverend Nate and Angie laughed good naturedly before the pastor continued: 'As you can see, we have picnic tables set up everywhere. I'm told the food will be ready in about thirty minutes, so let's enjoy each other's company – and don't worry, I'll tell you when we are ready to eat!'

Several children ran toward Jeremy Wilcox wanting to look at the camera. The journalist held each one up, allowing them to look through the camera's lenses. When the last kid had departed, Jeremy turned and saw the marshal standing behind him.

'I've got a little favor to ask,' Shem Carson said. 'But it's a favor you're gonna like.'

'Sounds like you're giving this reporter good news, Marshal.'

The lawman briefly looked at the ground in a gesture of embarrassment. 'I know I've been a bit ornery with you. But havin' all those stories about Coyote in the New York papers…well…it could outright ruin a town like Conrad. We need folks to move here, start ranches and businesses. Nobody's gonna move to a town where some spook is killin' off the population.'

'News is news, Marshal.'

'Yep, and like I said, I've got good news: we've captured the man who's done all the Coyote killings!'

'What…ah…who!?'

A proud grin cut across the lawman's face. 'Akando: he's admitted to it.'

'Well…why would Akando do it?'

'We don't know all that yet.' Carson gave a contemptuous snort. 'Akando is in rough shape. He's semi-conscious at best, with a broken nose. But he'll be talkin' soon. I got him in jail.' The marshal lowered his voice as if telling an off-colour joke. 'I put him in the middle cell between Howard Dixon and Vince Bursey, serves them buzzards right!'

'Congratulations, Marshal,' Jeremy appeared confused. 'About that favor…'

The lawman smiled at his own forgetfulness. 'Oh, yeh! Once the picnic really gets goin' I'm gonna announce about Akando. That will make it official. Could you write up a story for the New York paper, let 'em know Conrad is once ag'in a safe and peaceful place? You can take a picture of Akando if you'd like.'

'Of course!'

'Thanks!' Shem Carson slapped the journalist on his back. 'Havin' a newspaper in Conrad is a great thing! Sorry I've been sorta harsh with you in the past.'

A loud voice carried over the crowd. 'Food's ready, come and get it!'

'We better get movin' before the really good stuff is all gone,' Carson said.

Wilcox shook his head. 'I need to get this camera back to the office…away from the kids.'

'Guess that contraption cost plenty!' Carson looked appreciatively at the contraption.

'It sure wasn't cheap.'

'Don't take too long,' the marshal waved as he headed for the food table.

The smile vanished from Jeremy Wilcox's face the moment he turned and began to walk toward the newspaper office. He had known something was wrong when the wedding ceremony began. Sahale was the best man, and Sahale was supposed to be dead. But Wilcox had assumed that their gamble hadn't worked. Sahale hadn't stopped to water his horse.

So, what really had happened? Wilcox increased the pace of his steps as his mind frantically scrambled for answers. Sahale must have stopped to water his horse after all. But Akando had botched his most important performance as Coyote. Sahale had overwhelmed the renegade, beaten him all to hell, and dragged him to a prison cell.

Jeremy unlocked the door to this office, hurried in, put the camera in a closet, and then placed both hands on his desk. He closed his eyes and took several deep breaths.

All was not lost…hell…nothing was lost…not yet, he thought. Akando had said nothing to incriminate him. The stupid Indian was too beaten up to talk.

Wilcox opened the bottom drawer of his desk and pulled out a Smith and Wesson .44. He checked the cylinders to make sure the gun was loaded. Akando was a bitter man who wouldn't hesitate to drag his boss to the gallows with him.

Jeremy yanked a shoulder holster from the open drawer and then slammed it shut with his foot. Akando was about to be shot and killed while in his cell. Wilcox couldn't blame this killing on Coyote, but he would come up with some theory to put the law on a long trail to nowhere. From the conversation he had just had with the marshal, it was obvious that the lawman held him in high regard. Jeremy felt a wave of contentment. That high regard could be exploited.

The reporter hurriedly removed his coat and strapped on the shoulder holster. Putting the coat back on, he looked around the office, scooped up an old crate and left through the back door.

Taking the back road was little more than a precaution. The whole town was at the picnic. There was no one around to spot the curious sight of a reporter carrying a crate to the marshal's office.

Jeremy slowed his steps as he reached the office which was located at the end of the street. There were three barred windows on the far side of the office. They all looked out on a small field consisting of four trees, brown grass and a few bushes struggling in the hot sun. Wilcox's professional duties had brought him to the marshal's office many times. He was certain each window only allowed for a very limited sideways view. Still, he pulled a bandanna from one pocket and tied it around the bottom half of his face.

'This has to be fast,' the reporter whispered to himself. He needed to get back to the picnic soon. Before doing anything else, he would bestow effusive compliments on the ladies for the delicious food. He'd tell them he had stuffed himself, chatter on about each item and create confusion as to how long he had been there.

Bending into a jack-knife position, Wilcox moved to the middle window. He placed the crate on the ground and stood on it. Luck was still with him! Akando lay sleeping or unconscious on the cot.

Wilcox fired a bullet into the limp figure. Shocked by what he saw, he pumped a second shot hoping it would prove his eyes wrong. There was no one on the cot, only a collection of blankets and rags.

'I've been set up!' A storm of panic enveloped the reporter as his eyes scanned the field and spotted nothing. He saw the livery, which stood on the other side of the street about twenty yards away. Escape, yes, his only hope now was escape.

*

Rance Dehner stood behind one of the four trees that formed a bent half circle at the end of the field that was alongside the marshal's office. The detective had to stand erect in a sideways stance, otherwise the tree wouldn't cover his body. Two other trees covered men in similar positions: Stacey Hooper was behind one of them, and Rip Gowdy behind another. Shem Carson had remained at the picnic in case their theory was wrong and there was trouble of some kind at the church.

The three men occasionally exchanged smiles, realizing an outside observer would think them ridiculous. The smiles vanished when they saw a masked figure approach the center barred window with a crate in hand.

Dehner drew his gun, remembering Shem Carson's instructions. 'You and Hooper are there for back-up. Let Gowdy handle any trouble, he's the guy most folks in town regard as a lawman.'

The detective tensed as Wilcox fired two shots into the cell. The gunman suddenly turned and began to run at a surprising speed. Wilcox was almost out of the field when Rip Gowdy stepped from behind a tree and fired a warning shot into the air. 'Stop, or I'll shoot to kill!'

What happened next stunned all three of Wilcox's supposed captors. While still running, Jeremy Wilcox quickly turned in a panicked manner and fired his gun without aiming. By all rational standards the bullet should have whined into the air harmlessly. But that didn't happen. Rip Gowdy yelled in pain as he let go of his Colt, stumbled backwards, and then flopped to the ground.

Stacey Hooper ran to the fallen deputy. 'I'll look after him.' He gestured for Rance to go after the killer.

Rance complied. Wilcox once again turned and fired recklessly, this time at Dehner who had started the chase as a distant figure but was moving with what Wilcox regarded as a terrifying speed. But luck had abandoned Jeremy Wilcox: this time his shot burrowed into the ground, closer to him than his pursuer.

That failure heightened Wilcox's panic. The killer ripped the bandanna from his face to help his breathing, and then ran through the open double doors of Higgin's Livery and Blacksmith.

Rance slowed his pace as he neared the livery. The building was dark inside, with very little sunlight gleaming between the wooden planks. 'Conrad *would* have to have one of the best constructed livery and blacksmith operations in Texas,' Dehner whispered, amused at the irony.

The detective pressed himself against one of the large double doors that was open against the front of the building. He looked inside and didn't see any indication of where Wilcox might be hiding.

There was an advantage to this situation, Dehner thought. If Wilcox tries to escape through a back door, a huge shaft of light will betray his move.

The detective cautiously moved into the doorway so that his body was partially visible from inside. 'You're in a lot of trouble, Jeremy. Don't make things worse. Throw down your gun and surrender.'

Rance was hoping his adversary would attempt a shot at him and reveal his location. But that didn't happen. Dehner retreated to his former position and mulled over what he had just seen.

The inside of Higgin's Livery and Blacksmith was as tidy as such an operation could possibly be. Long rows of stalls lined the back area on each side of the back double door. The left front of the building was occupied by a forge.

A hayloft ran across the left side of the building, at a safe distance back from the forge. The detective reckoned Mr Higgin probably rented out that loft as a place where a weary traveler who couldn't afford a hotel could bed down for the night. But on this Sunday afternoon the loft was, in all likelihood, the hiding place for a murderer.

Rance stepped closer to the open doorway and again peered inside. On the right side of the building, near the front doors, stood two rows of tightly packed bales of hay, four bales in each row. Could two bales of hay stop a bullet fired from a pistol?

'Guess there's only one way to find out,' Dehner mused out loud as he ran inside and took cover behind the bales.

Dehner figured he had already used the proper approach to getting Wilcox to surrender. Now it was time to get personal.

'Hey, Jeremy, come on out and give yourself up; you've got nothing to worry about,' the detective shouted in a mock friendly voice. 'You see, I know the truth about you. Your momma died when you were in diapers and your daddy was busy making lots of money, so you were raised by the hired help.'

There was no response to Dehner's words. The detective knew he had to press harder. 'But your pap is really a pretty decent sort. He felt guilty about ignoring you. So he did the only thing he could do, he spent a lot of money on his son. Nothing was too good for his boy. He sent you to the very best schools and wrapped you in a lot of expensive clothes.'

The detective thought he heard some stirring from up in the hayloft, but he couldn't place the location with any accuracy. 'After you finished college you wanted to be a newspaper reporter, didn't you Jeremy? But no newspaper would hire you. So Daddy bought a newspaper for his little boy. Only little Jeremy wasn't very good at taking criticism. You punched an editor, who then fired you. You placed your pap in an impossible situation. He couldn't defend you, so he did the next best thing.'

'Shut your damn mouth!'

The words came out as a high-pitched squeak. Wilcox sounded like he was crying.

Dehner kept pushing. 'Daddy gave his son a lot of money and told him to head out west and start his own newspaper. He was probably hoping the West would turn you into a strong man. Jeremy Wilcox, a strong man – what a joke!'

This time the stirring was louder, and Rance had a good idea of his adversary's location. Wilcox might be positioning himself to fire over the straw bales. But Jeremy Wilcox was an anguished man, and that didn't bode well for long-distance accuracy.

The detective moved to his final thrust. 'So, like I said, Jeremy, you've got nothing to fret over. Your pap will buy the best lawyers in the country and send them out here to defend you. Daddy's not going to allow his little boy to...'

'Go to hell, Rance Dehner!' Wilcox rose to his knees and fired twice. The straw bales absorbed both shots, but Wilcox couldn't see that. Rance knew he was dealing with a frantic, unbalanced man and opted not to fire back.

The detective pretended to screech in pain, then cursed loudly and stumbled, bent over, out of the building. He continued to bellow when he was outside, dropping to the ground in the loudest manner possible. He then quietly jumped up, moved to the doorway and looked inside.

Jeremy Wilcox was scrambling down the ladder that leaned against the loft. As his feet touched the ground he ran toward the stalls. There was no gun in his hand.

Holstering his Colt, Dehner entered the livery and moved quietly toward Wilcox. The newspaperman headed for a stall with a saddle draped across a side wall, thinking his adversary was lying wounded outside. He had just placed his hands on the saddle when calm whispered words sounded behind him.

'It's all over, Jeremy. Turn around and put your hands up.'

Wilcox twisted his body in a half-turn, one arm reaching for his gun. Dehner delivered a hard right fist to the side of the killer's head. A loud thud filled the livery as Wilcox's body slammed against the stall, and the horse inside thrust its head up with a nervous snort.

Wilcox plunged face first on to the ground, but he lifted himself on to his side and started to pull his Smith and Wesson from its shoulder holster. Dehner grabbed the gun and tossed it into the darkness of the livery.

'You're not so good at doing your own killing, are you, Jeremy?' Dehner was surprised by the bitterness in his own voice. 'You need to pay for that service.'

For a moment, the murderer said nothing. He seemed to be giving Dehner's last statement serious thought. He then lifted up a hand as if beckoning the detective to help him up. Dehner grabbed the killer's arm and held on to it until Wilcox was steady on his feet.

A broad, desperate smile cut across Wilcox's face. 'How much does that agency you work for pay, Rance?'

'Enough.'

'I'll more than double it! Come into the newspaper game with me.'

Dehner felt oddly chilled by the man who had an increasingly crazy look on his face. 'You're done in the newspaper game.'

'It doesn't have to be that way!' The killer quickly glanced about the livery as if looking for possible witnesses as he dropped his voice to a whisper. 'You've killed men, haven't you, Rance? Hell, you've done some killing right here in Conrad.'

Dehner nodded his head.

Wilcox's voice remained a frantic whisper. 'Kill Akando! I don't know where the damn Indian is, but you do! I was masked when I fired those shots into the jail. We'll tell people the culprit got away, but that Akando was the Coyote killer. I can come up with a great story and make you the hero. Hell, I'm great at thinking up stories…'

The killer began to talk faster, scrambling his words together while his eyes seemed to bulge, giving his face an aura of madness. Rance watched, stunned, as he realized Jeremy Wilcox was performing a macabre impersonation of the father he hated and wanted to best. Jeremy's father had thought he could buy off the guilt that came from neglecting his son. Jeremy was certain that dollars could atone for mass murder. He only had to find the right price.

Jeremy continued to babble as Dehner led him to jail.

CHAPTER TWENTY-NINE

A dying sun splattered blood-red patches on to the floor of the Red Eye Saloon. A small scattering of customers dotted the establishment. The bartender quickly carried a glass of water to a table near the bar where Shem Carson and Rance Dehner were helping Rip Gowdy sit down while Stacey Hooper steadied the chair.

'I don't need all this fuss,' Gowdy complained. 'That bullet only grazed me.'

'From what I unnerstand, you lost a lot of blood,' Harry spoke as he placed the glass in front of Rip. 'Drink this, it's the best thing for you.'

'Do what the man says!' Carson declared. 'You're dealing with the new manager of both the Red Eye and Lucky Ace saloons.'

'Congratulations, sir!' Stacey beamed.

Harry shrugged his shoulders. 'Guess Mister Freemont, the banker, didn't have much choice. Sam is dead and Howard Dixon is in jail. Hope I can make a good job of it.'

'You will,' Stacey assured him. 'But I do advise that you do not do business with a Mr Charlie Bell.'

Harry smiled and nodded as he headed to the area behind the bar where food was prepared. The marshal looked a tad sheepish as the three men who were still standing at the table sat down. 'I'm going to close Charlie Bell down, tomorrow,' the lawman explained.

'Ya gonna arrest him?' Rip Gowdy asked as he sipped the water.

'Naaa, I don't think so,' Carson answered. 'I've been talkin' with Akando and I'm pretty sure Charlie knew nothin' 'bout all the killin's. He was only caught up in a big moonshine operation. I'm orderin' him to leave the area and not come back.'

The marshal shifted his eyes between Rance and Stacey. 'You gents already ran poor Charlie outta Conrad.'

'We had no choice,' Dehner acknowledged. 'Charlie showed up in town yesterday. If he'd found out that Stacey didn't own the Red Eye he could have started asking questions and ruined everything. We were able to get Honey to help us.'

'And my acting skills once again came into good use,' Stacey added immodestly. 'My impersonation of Jeremy Wilcox's voice was absolutely perfect. Rance performed the more mundane task of shoving poor Charlie out the door.'

'The tie-in between Bell and Wilcox became apparent right after Sam and Lafe got themselves killed,' Dehner added.

'How's that?' the marshal asked.

'Remember when we were standing outside Ma Trent's Restaurant and Jeremy pulled up in the middle of the street to tell us Howard Dixon was talking to the banker?'

'Well yeh, Rance, but...'

The detective continued: 'Jeremy's horse had been ridden hard. That night, Bell told me he knew Sam and Lafe were dead. The moonshiner rarely came into town, so how did he know? That news had shocked Wilcox and he felt he needed to share it, right away, with Charlie Bell. When we saw him and his tired horse, he was just getting back.'

Shem nodded his head as he listened appreciatively to steaks sizzling in the background. 'Reverend Nate and his bride should be here soon for our dinner.'

'They were just married a few hours ago,' Stacey said, 'you would think they'd have more interesting things to do.'

'Stacey, you…'

Whatever admonition Rance had in mind for his friend was stopped by the entrance of the couple. The four men at the table stood up, which caused Angie to put her hands on Rip's shoulders and guide him back into his chair. A few minutes of jokes followed and then everyone sat down as Harry brought out the food.

'We really are famished,' Reverend Nate explained. 'All day we were surrounded by delicious food but too busy talking to people to have time to eat.'

Angie playfully slapped her husband's arm. 'Don't be such a grouch! The people were very kind and the day was wonderful.'

'Yes,' Nate agreed, 'the day was wonderful.'

The bride gave a magnificent smile as she looked at her husband and then at the other men at the table. 'Most children get bored and fussy when their mother talks about her wedding day, but I'll be able to tell my kids and grandkids that I helped trap a killer on my wedding day, and I owe it all to you gentlemen. Only, I'm a bit confused about the details, could you fill me in?'

Shem spoke as he began to cut his steak. 'Yeh Rance, what got you suspicious of Jeremy Wilcox?'

154

'In a way, Jeremy did,' the detective responded. 'Jeremy told me there had been no reports of a large number of Winchesters being stolen. That meant the rifles given to the Indians had been purchased, illegally probably, but in a way that wouldn't alert the law, and that wouldn't have been cheap.'

Dehner paused to organize his thoughts. 'In fact, large sums of money kept popping up in this case. Those bottles Charlie Bell is using for his moonshine operation are the very best, as is the press he employs to make the labels. So, where is the loot coming from?'

'Jeremy Wilcox!' Stacey exclaimed. 'Why, he bragged about the first-rate press he has for his newspaper, and even carried on about an expensive camera. I find it highly unlikely that advertising from local merchants could pay for such elaborate tools.'

'You're right,' Rance agreed. 'But Jeremy needed the advertising to provide him with cover. He didn't want people getting too curious about where the dollars really came from.' Dehner then explained how Wilcox's father had provided him with money to atone for the years of neglecting his son.

'But, why?' the bride's voice sounded like a plea. 'Why kill so many innocent people?'

'Money,' Dehner answered. 'Wilcox planned to be even richer than his daddy.'

The groom shook his head. 'I'm still in the dark. How could killing a poor man like Leo or a struggling rancher like Pete Clement make anyone rich?'

'They were killed in order to make people believe in the reality of Coyote,' Dehner said. 'Leo was killed in front of Gerald, a man who scared easily and talked a lot. Pete's wife Mona is known for being very superstitious. Akando killed Leo and Pete. He was following Jeremy's instructions, though he carried out the murders at his own convenience. He probably wore a hood over his head, a duster and a wide-brimmed hat to cover his identity. Jeremy Wilcox was certain there were enough superstitious people around, both townspeople and Indians, that when the news of the murders spread, a lot of people would believe the Coyote myth.'

'And he was right,' Reverend Nate's voice conveyed sadness. 'But how could it benefit Wilcox to have a lot of folks believing in Coyote?'

'The goal was to kill Sahale,' Dehner paused, allowing that statement to sink in. 'Jeremy immediately pegged Akando as wanting power, but not knowing how to achieve it. Wilcox knew that if Sahale were to be killed, Akando would be the most obvious suspect. So Wilcox had Akando kill Leo and Pete Clement, beginning Coyote's reign of terror and confusion. Sahale's murder would be just another Coyote killing.'

'Yeh, but,' Rip Gowdy finished his last sip of water and put the empty cup down, 'how would killin' Sahale help Wilcox to get rich?'

'Fort Williamson is expanding. They're going to need a lot of horses. Akando and his braves were going to provide them and quickly eliminate any competition from other tribes, probably by using Coyote.' Dehner sighed in a resigned manner. 'Of course, Wilcox would have gotten a cut from all sales. Jeremy was confident that he could keep Akando under his control.'

'How did Charlie Bell fit into all of this?' Shem asked.

A wistful look came over the detective's face. 'One of the sad truths in this case is that Jeremy Wilcox really did have the makings of a good journalist. When he arrived in Conrad and set up shop, he went looking for good stories. That's how he connected with Akando.'

'And it is also how he encountered Mister Charlie Bell,' Stacey added.

'Right,' Dehner replied. 'Charlie was just a moonshiner with big ideas. Wilcox gave him the money to make those ideas a reality. In return, he got a fat cut of the profits. Wilcox also persuaded Akando to provide Charlie with workers: workers who would keep quiet. But Sahale would never tolerate the use of young Indians as moonshiners. Another reason he had to be killed.'

'What's going to happen next?' Angie asked in a whisper.

'Charlie is leaving for good, Wilcox and Akando are bein' charged with murder and...'

'You are correct about all that, Marshall,' Nate said. 'But there is much more. A lot of hate and distrust has come out because of Coyote. A lot of good has also come to the surface. We must see that the good prevails.'

Angie's voice remained a whisper. 'It's going to be a big job.'

'Yes,' Stacey agreed. 'But first we have a marvelous dinner in front us and two wonderful people to toast and wish a happy journey in their life together!'

Cheer and laugher followed.

*

Two hours later, Rance and Stacey stood on the boardwalk outside the Red Eye, watching their dinner companions depart. 'I've been answering questions all evening, Stacey. Now, it's your turn.'

'Always happy to enlighten you, my friend, what exactly is the nature of your inquiry?'

'Why were you so anxious to have *me* get involved in this whole Coyote matter?'

Stacey sighed deeply and looked toward the sky. 'You will just never understand my deep desire to follow the example of the Good Samaritan and…'

'Stacey!'

'Well, there were some secondary considerations.'

'Such as?'

'On the Sunday night before your arrival I placed quite a few bets with the locals. It seemed that some confused souls believed what Akando had babbled in the church that morning about Coyote. I bet them Coyote was a myth, and that there would be no attacks by a savage, supernatural beast. I thought it would be easy money, and of course, steer some poor misled individuals from their superstitious ways.'

'And then Leo was murdered and Gerald starting shouting about Coyote.'

The gambler nodded his head. 'That all happened less than a half hour after I had placed my final wager…quite awkward.'

Dehner stood silent for a moment, absorbing what his friend had just said. 'But there couldn't have been that much money involved.'

A triumphant smile suddenly dominated Stacey's face. 'Tonight I am giving you an important insight into the mind of the gambler, or at least, this gambler. I'm not driven by money alone. No, equally important, or almost as important, is winning. If I had ended up paying out money to a dozen or so superstitious fools, my soul would have been forever damaged.'

Rance looked unconvinced. Stacey Hooper pressed his case. 'How much money did you make unmasking this Coyote nonsense and risking your life in the process?'

'None,' Dehner admitted.

Hooper raised an index finger in victory. 'Exactly! For you, the equivalent of winning is getting to the truth, wherever it takes you. In your case, that is far more important than the accumulation of filthy lucre!'

Dehner conceded, 'You win.'

'Exactly the words I wanted to hear. Now that we have finished with business, we shall move on to pleasure. When do you want to go fishing tomorrow?'

Dehner shook his head. 'Another time. I'm heading back to Dallas at sun-up. I've already tested the patience of my boss.'

'So, the poor dumb creatures who populate the streams of Conrad are also winners. They are safe from two of the West's finest fishermen.' Stacey waved a thumb backwards toward the Red Eye. 'On the subject of poor dumb creatures, I spotted some men who owe me money scattered about the saloon. I must attend to business.'

'Stacey, don't you feel a bit guilty about collecting money on bets made with gullible bar flies?'

The gambler responded with a hearty laugh. 'Why should I? After all, I intend to stay in town for another week and give them a chance to win it back. I hope our trails cross again soon, good friend!' Stacey continued to laugh as he re-entered the saloon.

*

To his own surprise, Rance didn't leave Conrad at sun-up the next morning. He found himself dawdling over break-fast, and then before leaving town, he paused his bay on a knoll near the school where, with the help of field glasses, he watched the scene unfolding nearby. Both Indian chil-dren and the children of the townspeople and ranchers were arriving for their classes. But they no longer required armed guards.

Reverend Nate and Angie were bustling about welcom-ing the kids. *The newlyweds aren't having much of a honeymoon, but they certainly look happy,* the detective mused to himself.

Sahale accompanied the Indian children. Reverend Nate had told his companions the previous night that Sahale wanted to talk to the children about the monstrous Coyote: how Coyote is makebelieve, but that some bad people used superstition for their own selfish reasons. 'We need to close the door on all the terrible things that have happened in this town,' Nate had said.

Dehner knew the pastor had been right. He also knew the closed door eliminated any need for him. Still, he allowed himself one final glimpse at the joyous spectacle. Stacey Hooper had a point, winning can be wonderful, and Rance Dehner felt he was watching people who had won a very important battle.

The detective returned the field glasses to his saddle bag and rode off into the warmth of a new day's sun.